THE SUMERIAN CURSE

THE SUMERIAN CURSE

LEIGH ANDERSON

For dear reader Ilene Todd, who gave me the idea for this book.

Red Empress Publishing
www.RedEmpressPublishing.com

Cover by Sanja Gombar
https://www.facebook.com/groups/883123058528414

ALSO BY LEIGH ANDERSON

Urban Fantasy

Pirate's Curse

Sword Kissed

Gothic Romances

The Creation of Eve

Dangerous Passions

The Sumerian Curse

The Calmet Chronicles

The Vampire's Gift

The Vampire's Daughter

The Vampire's Slayer

The Vampire's Lover

The Shifters of Africa

The Lioness of Egypt

The Pride of Egypt

The Queen of Egypt

PREFACE

The "Sumerian" translations in this book are loosely,
loosely, loosely based on Sumerian and Akkadian words,
but for the most part are completely made up and probably
gibberish. The Arabic, however, I hope is correct. But if my
Arabic translations could be improved, please let me know.

CHAPTER ONE

*E*velyn ran her fingers over the fine silk scarves for sale in the marketplace. Every color imaginable, from the pale creams and pinks to vibrant deep purples and reds formed a rainbow on the merchant's table.

"A beautiful scarf for a beautiful little lady, *aanesa*," the Arabic man with kind eyes said as he wiggled his mustache at her.

"*Kam yukalif?*" she replied. *How much*, in Arabic.

The man laughed. "*Hal tatakalam Alearabia?*" *You speak Arabic?* "*Balnsbt lk, sier khasun jidanaan.*" *For you, a very special price.*

Evelyn smiled and blushed, proud of how far her language skills had progressed in the two years she had been living in Persia—not to mention her bargaining prowess. She was able to easily converse with locals, not quite at a native level, but fluently enough that people took her seriously when she spoke to them.

She was very near to getting an excellent price on two of the scarves when she felt a hand on her arm.

"Don't waste your time with these swindlers," her father

said, rudely pulling her away from the stall. "They'll rip you off as soon as look at you."

"But, Papa, I—" she tried to explain as she shot the merchant an apologetic look.

"If you need something, just have Marcus order it for you," he went on, dragging her through the market. "He has the best contacts in the city."

Actually, from what Evelyn had seen, Marcus, Lord Graham, was viewed by the locals as an easy mark. Everything doubled and tripled in price when he walked anywhere near a shop. But Evelyn bit her tongue and kept her words to herself on that score.

"It wasn't about the money," Evelyn said, which was a lie, "but about practicing my Arabic."

"Don't you have a tutor for that?" he asked as he slowed down to admire a woman selling hand-woven rugs.

"Yes," Evelyn said. "But practicing in a classroom isn't the same as conversing with people on the street."

Her father smiled at the woman, lost in his own little world. The woman bent over to smooth out a rug that was already far smooth enough and gave Evelyn's father a wink.

"My rugs are the best for British exporting," the woman purred at him.

"I'm sure they are," her father said, stepping closer to examine the woman's...wares.

Evelyn rolled her eyes and tugged at her father's arm. "Papa!" she said harshly. "If I'm not allowed to be ripped off by the market sellers, you shouldn't be either!"

"Huh?" he asked, coming out of his daze. "What? Oh, right. Come along." He continued walking, tugging Evelyn along. "What were we talking about? Right. Commoners! That's all these people are. Worse than commoners. Back in

England would your mother have let you run down to Trent Street and haggle with the fishmongers?"

Evelyn sighed. "No," she said. But that was one of the reasons she loved living in Persia. The rules that governed strict British society weren't enforced here.

"Quite right," her father said. "Now, come with me."

"Where are we going?" she asked as they exited the market and climbed into a man-pulled cart.

"To the dig site," he said. He tried to tell the cart driver where to go, but the man did not understand her father's butchered Arabic. Evelyn cleared her throat and told the driver where to go. "That's my girl," her father said, proudly wrapping his arm around her shoulder.

"I get to go to the site?" Evelyn asked, perking up. Normally, she wasn't allowed to visit the dig site. It was considered too dangerous for her to go. She was left behind in the safety of the guesthouse to her own devices. And while she didn't mind the freedom such a life afforded her, she often missed her father and wished he would let her be a part of what he so enjoyed—digging up ancient artifacts from around the world.

"We've discovered something rather extraordinary," her father said. "But the locals, superstitious fools that they are, refuse to tell what the carvings mean. I told them they could just bugger off. I had the best translator of ancient Sumerian back in my hotel room."

"Aww, Papa," Evelyn said, her heart swelling. Of course, coming from a man who could hardly even tell ancient Sumerian from ancient Egyptian, the praise was rather empty. But studying ancient Near East iconography had become a hobby she had picked up over the few years since she started traveling with her father. Truth be told, even her limited understanding of Sumerian *was* impressive, even by local Persian standards considering that Sumerian had not been an active language for centuries.

As they approached the dig site, the area was abuzz with people, camels, dogs, and equipment. Local men wearing only pants and soft-soled shoes hastily carried baskets of sand away from the area, their chests and backs gleaming with sweat. The sight of people wearing far less clothing here shocked Evelyn when she had first arrived, but now she hardly gave it a second thought. It didn't take long for her governess to start stripping layers out of their own clothes to make them more tolerable in the desert heat. The governess didn't last long even after that adjustment.

Evelyn stood up in the cart and looked out over the endless desert before stepping down. From her slightly elevated vantage point, the majesty of the landscape nearly took her breath away. The slowly undulating dunes in every shade of yellow and brown reflected the sunlight in rays of pink, orange, and purple. She wished her father had given her some notice of their trip today so she could have brought her drawing kit.

"Miss Evelyn?" a young man called up to her, holding out his hand.

Evelyn was called out of her daydreaming and smiled down at him. She gave him her hand and he helped her out of the cart.

"Hamid," she said. "Good to see you again."

"Come along, Evie," her father called as he headed into the camp.

"*What brings you out here today*?" Hamid asked her in Arabic as he walked alongside her.

"*Papa says he has something Sumerian for me to translate*," she replied in kind.

Hamid stopped suddenly, gripping her arm. She was

forced to stop walking and face him. Her smile quickly fled when she saw the fear on his face.

"No, Miss Evelyn," he said in English, clearly for her benefit so she would not mistake his meaning.

"What's wrong?" she asked.

"The cave," he said. "It is too dangerous. It is...*maleun*."

It took a moment for Evelyn to translate the word she had not heard often. "Cursed?" she finally asked.

"Yes, Miss Evelyn," he said with a nod. "Cursed."

"Evie!" her father called. "Stop conversing with that ruffian and let's go! The others are waiting."

Evelyn sighed and continued after her father, with Hamid closely behind. Hamid was the son of one of the local advisors for the British investors on the dig project. He had been instrumental in her early days of getting adjusted to life in the desert and had been her first language tutor. But as he had gotten older, his father wanted him by his side more to learn the family business, so they spent far less time together. But when it came to her questions about Persian language and culture, there was no one she trusted more than Hamid.

As they approached the entrance of the main dig site, her father descended the exposed stairs without a second thought. But Hamid hesitated, once again gripping Evelyn's elbow.

"*Do not go down there*," he said, returning to Arabic.

"*Are you making a joke at my expense*?" she asked.

"*I promise I am not*," he said, and she could see the sincerity in his eyes.

She glanced around and noticed that many of the locals had stopped working and were watching her with concern on their faces. She felt a cool breeze billow up out of the cave.

"You must be the famous Miss Evelyn Crowley," a man said as he stepped between her and Hamid and wrapped an arm around her shoulder, ushering her toward the cavern. "Your father has told me much about you."

As they stepped toward the entrance, a deep sense of foreboding washed over her, as though she was heading toward a lion's mouth. She dug her feet into the sand to stop herself from being forced any further.

"Evelyn!" her father shouted, popping back through the entrance. "What's going on? Ah! I see you've found Ol' Banning. He's quite keen to know what you think about the carvings. Come on." He waved her forward as he descended the steps again.

Evelyn sighed, the sense of fear having passed by as the man her father called Banning entered the cavern as well. She looked back toward Hamid and shrugged before following after the men. Whatever had Hamid spooked she would just have to see for herself.

The stairwell was quite dark, as there were no torches lining it. The ceiling was much too low so she had to crouch as the descended the stairs. But as she emerged into the first antechamber, the gasped at the sight. Torches lit up a room twenty-feet tall at least and dozens of feet in diameter. The walls were completely covered with ancient Sumerian carvings.

She heard laughter as she gazed at the walls, her mouth agape.

"I told you she'd be shocked," her father said.

Evelyn looked around and saw that all the important members of the expedition, at least half a dozen rich British and American men, were there. Well, important *foreign* members of the expedition. None of the local Persian experts or dignitaries were present.

"What's going on?" Evelyn asked.

"We were hoping you could tell us," the Banning said. "The local translators ran out of here screaming something about an evil curse."

"Primitive savages," another man said. "Can never trust them."

"We pay them far too much," another chimed in.

Evelyn pressed her lips. She hated the way many of her fellow Englishmen and woman spoke about the local people—people she had never known to be anything except kind of welcoming to her.

"Forget them," her father said. "This is clearly an important discovery. We need someone we can trust anyway."

"Trust...for what?" Evelyn asked.

"To translate, of course," her father said with a chuckle, motioning to the walls.

Evelyn looked at the walls again and sighed in frustration. "It's not that easy. Where do I even begin and end?"

"Just pick a spot," her father said.

Evelyn shook her head but did as her father said. "Walking...river...clawed eagle..." she said, reading off some of the characters she recognized.

"What does that mean?" one of the men interrupted.

"I don't know," Evelyn said. "I need time. Context. What is this place?"

"Show her the book," Banning said, ignoring her question.

The men all moved out of the way, forming a path toward the back of the chamber. On a pedestal was an extremely old book. She walked toward it and stepped up onto a crate in front of it to get a better look. The pages were frail and darkened with age. She was afraid to touch it lest the papyrus crumble in her hands.

This book was written in a language she was not familiar with. Well, there were similarities to ancient Sumerian, but they were scant. She had a feeling the book was written in a language even older than Sumerian.

"I...I can't," she said.

The men all groaned in annoyance.

"What?" one of them asked. "Not a thing?"

"It...it's not the Sumerian I am familiar with," she said.

Her father stepped up behind her and placed his hands on her shoulders. "Come now, Evie," he said. "Just try."

She looked back at the book, but she didn't know what he wanted from her. It wasn't possible to translate something she had never seen before. But as her eyes scanned the pages, she landed on one word she knew.

"*Utuk...xul...*" she mumbled.

"What does that mean?" Banning asked.

Evelyn looked at him. "Evil," she said.

The men all went silent and looked from one to another. Suddenly, a strong wind picked up and swirled around the cavern, kicking up the sand and causing them all to start coughing and choking.

Evelyn lifted her sleeve to her face. "Papa!" she called, her eyes watering and blurring her vision.

She felt someone grab her arm and lead her away from the book. She stumbled as she stepped off the crate, but she kept going. She heard the men around her yelling and panicking as they too were disoriented by the sand. She stubbed her toe on the first step to exit the cavern, but at least she knew she had been led in the right direction.

She scrambled up the stairs and flew out of the cave. The camp was in complete chaos. A sudden sandstorm seemed to have whipped up. While they were not uncommon, she had been lucky to never have been caught in one in the desert before, but had always been in the safety of the guesthouse.

She turned around, expecting to see her father, but it was Hamid who had led her out of the cavern.

"Hamid!" she cried, her voice becoming lost in the howling of the wind. "Papa! He's still down there!"

"I must get you to safety," he said.

"No!" she yelled. "My papa!"

She felt the hand of someone pulling her away. She looked up and saw Hamid's father.

"*We must hide!*" he yelled to his son in Arabic.

"*Take her!*" Hamid replied. "*I'll get the others!*"

"*No!*" his father yelled, but it was too late. Hamid had already disappeared back into the cave.

"Hamid!" Evelyn yelled, but his father was dragging her away toward a pit that was covered with a large leather tarp. Several other workers and their dogs had already taken cover in the pit, which had been dug and stocked with water, food, and shovels for just such a surprise storm. Nearby, camels bellowed as they were left to the elements, their owners having covered their eyes with leather blinders to protect them.

Hamid's father lowered Evelyn into the pit.

"No!" she cried. "Father! My father! Papa! Hamid!"

Hands from the other workers grabbed her and pulled her into the pit as Hamid's father then went back to the dig site to find his son.

"Papa! Papa!" Evelyn continued to scream as the tarp was lowered over her and she was enveloped in darkness.

CHAPTER TWO

"*E*velyn!" a voice called.

Evelyn gasped at being shaken from her bad memories. She had been dusting off an old Babylonian vase when she was suddenly transported back ten years previous to the day of her father's death.

"Evelyn?" Henry Wilkes asked. "Are you quite all right? You seem shaken."

Evelyn smiled and closed the door of the glass case that contained the vase. "I'm fine," she said. "Just...this wing of the museum always recalls to mind the years I spent in Persia."

Henry's nose wrinkled. "You don't have to come over here," he said. "There's scant interest in Persia nowadays. Egypt is all the rage."

"I've noticed," Evelyn said. The death of her father and the other lords at the dig site all those years ago put a sudden end to British excavation in Persia for the time being. The Persian government didn't want to be held responsible for another disaster and stopped issuing permission for foreign digs. Not that it stopped smugglers from going in and stealing occasional pieces, but the accident was considered a significant personal loss for the British. Many decided that the loss of so many great lords wasn't worth the cost of desert trinkets. Evelyn—as the sole foreign survivor of the accident—felt the loss more keenly than anyone. But then being unceremoniously banished from a place she had come to consider her adopted home was like salt on the wound. And when she returned to London, no one was interested in talking to her about her life there. Whenever she brought it up, she was given sad nods and pats on the back of the hand. She thought there was a balance to be found between losing life and limb to raid a country of its treasures and pretending the whole region simply didn't exist, but few seemed interested in hearing her thoughts on the matter. So, for the most part, she buried her feelings deep in a hole in her chest.

She cleared her throat and then motioned to the plaque on the vase's display case. "This description needs to be updated," she said. "It is certainly not from the first century. The Sumerian script is much older than that, perhaps by a thousand years."

"Bah," Henry said, placing his hand on her back and ushering her out of the Sumerian wing of the British Museum. "Not a priority at all. Come. Let's see what Lord Wenham has sent us."

Henry led Evelyn to the unboxing room of the museum where crates upon crates of Egyptian items had just arrived. Evelyn sighed at the daunting task ahead of them, but then bound up her long black hair, rolled back her sleeves, and grabbed a crowbar to open the first box. She coughed as she waved her hand in front of her face to clear the dust.

"What did you find?" Henry asked her.

Evelyn pulled out several small bronze jars that were ornately decorated.

"Lovely," she said as she went to grab her notebook so she could catalog the items as they were unpacked.

Henry picked up one of the jars and opened it. "What do you think they are? Snuff boxes?"

Evelyn took the jar from him and sniffed it. "It's for makeup."

Henry laughed. "Of course a lady would jump to such a conclusion."

"Do you see the reddish discoloration inside the jar?" she asked, holding it up so he could see. "And the smell? Those are not characteristics of tobacco, but henna." She opened another jar and saw that it was stained black inside. "See? Kohl. Eye makeup. Lip paint. Stains for cheeks. This is an ancient Egyptian noblewoman's makeup set."

"I knew there was a reason I kept you around," Henry teased, though Evelyn found it less than humorous. "Well, you keep working on this one and I'll get started over there. Hopefully we will have most of this at least unpacked before day's end."

The two worked in relative silence for the rest of the day, which more than suited Evelyn. Henry Wilkes was the curator for the ancient Near East and North African collections of the British Museum. When Evelyn returned from Persia, she had been given the enormous task of deciding what to do with her father's vast collection of items he had gathered from around the world. Even as a girl, she had worked closely with the museum owners to decide what to keep, what to donate, what to sell, and—in some cases—what to return to their country of origin. Even ten years later, she had not completed sorting through even half of her father's items.

She had already been working with the museum for years when Henry was hired. He was instantly smitten with her, she knew, though she was never particularly drawn to him. Even though he had studied ancient cultures at university, he had never left England. She found his understanding of Egyptian, Arabic, and Greek language and history to be superficial at best. As though someone who read *The Odyssey* was now suddenly in charge of the largest collection of Greek art in the world.

However, since Henry fancied her, he allowed her to not only work with him on her father's items, but he began taking her advice on other items the museum procured. He couldn't—or wouldn't, she wasn't exactly sure—give her a proper position, but he took her on an unofficial volunteer, allowing her to assist him with cataloging items, translating them, and writing their descriptions. She didn't mind doing the work on a voluntary basis. She didn't need the money. Though it irked her knowing that Henry took all the credit for her work. She watched silently as he received promotion after promotion and bathed in accolades from the museum's board of directors. While he had not been knighted, the Queen herself had praised the work he had done at the museum on behalf of the British Empire.

She had considered leaving the museum many times. Going back to working solely on her father's collection. But where would that leave her? Henry would likely end up losing his position and she'd be even worse off than before. As a woman—a lady, even—the museum would never hire her in her own right. And she'd lose the only ally who at least gave her access to all the wonderous items she loved so much.

The museum's collections were her only real connection to her lost childhood. When she was here, working with ancient texts, vases, reliefs, clothes, and so much more, she was transported back to the travels of her youth with her father. She could verily smell the sand and feel the heat of the sun on her skin.

It wasn't safe for a woman to travel alone, so since she was unmarried and didn't have a father, it was nearly unthinkable for her to be able to return to Persia. Until such a time as things changed—and she didn't see herself marrying anytime soon—having inside access to the museum's precious items was more important to her than money or accolades. So, while Henry was often condescending and patronizing, she simply smiled and nodded and kept on with a work that made her happy and filled a hole in her soul.

She hadn't even noticed how many hours had passed when Henry finally sighed and stretched his arms dramatically.

"What a day!" he said. "Fantastic work, Evelyn. We didn't get them all opened, but Monday for sure."

"Is it six o'clock already?" she asked, looking toward a window at the setting sun.

Henry laughed. "You need someone to go home to," he said. "Get your head out of your work sometimes."

"My maid, Susan, has been saying something similar," she said as she closed her notebook and put it in her bag.

"Oh?" Henry asked, raising an eyebrow.

"She is insisting we get a cat," she said.

"Oh," Henry said, disappointment clear in his voice. "Well, cats can be amiable companions, I suppose."

"So, I will see you Monday, then," Evelyn said.

"Actually," Henry said, "there is a little event here at the museum this weekend. I thought you might like to attend."

"An event?" Evelyn asked. "Why am I only hearing about it now?"

"Oh, it's nothing," Henry said—lied, more likely. "Just some of the museum's directors and their wives and a few other...people."

Evelyn raised her own eyebrow this time. This was not the first time Henry had "forgotten" to tell her about an event until the last minute. He would never admit it, but he knew she was more knowledgeable about the museum's collections than he was. If he knew an event centered around something he could talk about with at least some competence, he would conveniently forget to tell her about the event lest she speak up and look more informed than he. But sometimes an event centered around an item he certainly wouldn't be able to speak about on his own, so it would take him until the last possible moment to bury his pride enough to request her attendance.

"What is the event for?" Evelyn asked.

"Not what, but who. Jane Poole, Lady Grey," Henry said.

Evelyn's heart snagged in her chest. Jane Poole. She hadn't known Jane's father, Elmer Poole at the time, but he had been one of the men on the expedition who died along with her own father.

"She finally decided to donate some of the items her father collected before he died," Henry explained.

"She has?" Evelyn asked, suddenly...angry? Annoyed? Scared? She wasn't sure. But Henry should have known better than to keep something like this from her. "Why didn't you tell me?"

"I didn't see the need until it was finalized," Henry said. "You know no one is interested in Sumerian items right now. I didn't think the museum would want to dedicate any more space to them. But an anonymous donation came though earmarked for the Sumerian collection, so the directors accepted. I...I didn't want to upset you if the deal fell through. I was trying to protect you."

Now, Evelyn was angry. "You know how important the Sumerian collection is to me," she snapped as she grabbed her shawl and stomped toward the museum's front door.

"Evelyn," Henry said, exasperated as he followed on her heels. "I did what I thought was best."

"I should have been told the moment Jane Poole announced she wanted to part with those items," Evelyn said, pulling the heavy door open and letting the chilly evening air rush in.

"You don't *work* here, Evelyn," Henry said. "I don't answer to you—"

"Thank you for the reminder," she interrupted as she threw her shawl over her shoulders and stepped outside.

"But are you coming to the event or not?" Henry called out to her.

"You know I am!" she yelled over her shoulder.

"*Y*our Arabic is fantastic," an older man, Lord Bronn, said to Evelyn at the event the next evening. "I swear, if I close my eyes and listen to you, I would think I was back in Tunisia. But you have been safely here in London for so long. You must have an incredible memory."

Evelyn blushed at the compliment. "While I wish that were the case, I must admit that I have simply kept up with my studies since my return."

"And you speak Greek as well?" Lord Bronn asked.

"*Déchomai*," she said. *I do.*

Lord Bronn and a couple of other men who were listening to their conversation laughed.

"Brilliant!" Lord Bronn said. "Truly, a capable woman. How are you not married yet?"

"Unfortunately, until I meet a man who speaks at least eight languages, most men I know are far too intimidated by a woman who can ask them to put out their smelly cigars in seven," Evelyn said, reciting a quip that always sent men into peals of laughter. And this time was no different. The men laughed and clapped each other on the back as though they had made the joke.

"Such a waste of valuable time," came a cool voice from outside the group. The men parted, and Evelyn's breath hitched at the sight of Jane Poole. "When the people who speak a language have been dead for thousands of years, who are you going to talk to?"

The men chuckled halfheartedly and then scattered around the room to talk in quieter groups and avoid Jane's icy gaze.

Evelyn steeled herself as she approached Jane with an outstretched hand. "Lady Grey, Jane," she said, since they were of equal rank. "How nice to see you after so long."

"It's Lady Grant now," Jane said, not accepting Evelyn's offered hand, but instead reaching for a glass of wine from a footman.

"Forgive me," Evelyn said, clasping her hands in front of her. "I must have missed the announcement in the society page. But I am so happy to see you, and grateful for the donation of your father's items. I shall treasure studying them."

"It's complete garbage," Jane said. "I simply needed the room in my house it was all cluttering up. If the museum hadn't taken it, I'd have thrown it out on the street."

The room seemed to darken at Jane's words. Evelyn looked up and noticed that the gas lamps flickered, but they quickly returned to normal.

"If you have more items you wish to relinquish," Evelyn said, "I do hope you will give me the opportunity to claim them before you resort to such extremes."

"You talk to *me* of extremes?" Jane said through gritted teeth as she glared down at Evelyn. "Your *obsession* with these...*things* is what's extreme. Our fathers died scouring in the dirt for them. Even before they died, they abandoned us for years. I last saw my father when I was six years old! How can you waste your life following in their selfish footsteps?"

Evelyn nodded and accepted Jane's vitriol without responding in kind. The children of all the men who died in the accident had been brought together soon after the deaths of their fathers. Their mothers and guardians thought it would be good for them to lean on one another after a shared tragedy. But Evelyn had been the only one present at the accident, and one of the few who had been allowed to travel with her father at all. As a result, the other children seemed to see Evelyn as the only living target available for them to hurl their anger at. They saw Evelyn as one of *them*, an ally of their selfish fathers, as opposed to one of their own—a grieving little girl.

It hurt, being the target of such anger from people she had grown up with, people who shared her pain. But she didn't retaliate. She knew they were hurting as much as she was. She had once hoped that over time, the would realize the error of their ways in holding her accountable for their fathers' deaths, but it never happened. If anything, it got worse. She ended up shut out of most social circles. The London Season ended up being just as lonely for her as the rest of the year. And despite her wealth and title, she had never been courted. She wondered if the others saw her as some sort of curse. A woman of bad luck no one wanted in their family.

She had retreated further into her studies and her work at the museum, which seemed to only increase the ire of the other children—all, like Evelyn, of course, who were now adults—on the few occasions she happened to come into contact with them.

"Dedicating your life to something more than parties and expensive hats is never a waste," Henry said, stepping up.

"Henry—" Evelyn started to say but was interrupted.

"How dare you!" Jane erupted. "You were practically *begging* for my father's collection, and now you speak to me like this?"

"Evelyn is a valued member of the British Museum family," Henry said. "I'll brook no insult of her here."

"Please, Henry, you don't—" Evelyn tried again, but Henry held his hand up to quiet her.

"We appreciate your donation," Henry said to Jane. "But if this event in your father's honor brings you no joy, perhaps it should be at an end."

"By all means," Jane said, slamming her wine glass down on a footman's tray who was standing nearby. "Drink. Be merry. Party at the expense of my father's life. I don't care." She turned and walked out the front door of the museum, a man Evelyn could only assume was Jane's husband scurrying after her.

While Evelyn felt a small relief at Jane's departure, the whole encounter had shaken her.

Henry laid a hand on her shoulder. "I hope I put her in her place."

"You shouldn't have done that," Evelyn said in a harsh

whisper as she glanced around at the other guests who had apparently stopped to watch the women argue but were now returning to their own conversations.

"What?" Henry asked incredulously. "She was insulting you. I came to your defense."

"You don't understand the...situation," Evelyn said. "The history between Jane and me. You've just made things much worse."

Henry frowned and took a step back. "You know, a thank you wouldn't go amiss."

Evelyn scoffed and rolled her eyes as she pushed past him out of the room. She couldn't be near him right now. She hadn't asked for his assistance and he certainly didn't deserve a thank you. She knew that Jane was out of line. After so long, it was time Jane came to her senses. But that was a conversation for Evelyn and Jane to have—not Jane and Henry Wilkes.

"Evelyn!" Henry called, but she left the room, climbed up the stairs, and fled down the hall to the Sumerian wing. She closed the doors behind her and took a deep breath.

Once she had calmed down, she straightened her hair and her blouse and decided to take a turn about the room. She just needed a few minutes to collect her thoughts before she could even consider being near Henry right now. The Sumerian wing was like a second home to her. There was never anywhere else in London she would rather be than here.

Even though it was night and the room dark, low-burning gas lamps illuminated the room, enabling her to see the familiar displays. She walked past sculpted reliefs, household jars, cups and plates, and jewelry to stand in front of one of her favorite vases—one engraved with a winged ram rearing up on his hind legs. She had been there when her father discovered it, but she had never been able to discern its meaning. She had originally wanted to keep in her private collection, but she hoped that by displaying it, someone someday might see it who would be able to explain its significance to her.

As her eyes followed the ram's back up to the tips of his curved horns, her eyes readjusted and she gasped. In the glass, she was sure she saw the cloaked figure of a person standing behind her.

"Who's there?" she called as she turned around, but she did not see anyone. She stood completely silent save for her suddenly haggard breaths and rapidly beating heart. "Hello?" she finally called again after a moment.

She heard the door to the wing open and close quickly. Someone had been there! She ran toward the door and flung it open, hoping to catch a glimpse of whoever it was as he fled down the hall.

But when she looked, no one was there.

CHAPTER THREE

"*M*aybe it was a naughty couple who had slipped away from the event for a quick cuddle," Henry said with a laugh.

Evelyn shot him a look and then laughed as well. She was in the museum basement, in the records hall, compiling her notes for the opened crates from Lord Wenham into official museum inventory cards, when Henry found her on Monday afternoon. She had hidden in the basement to avoid having to face him after the upsetting events of the weekend, but Henry was never one to leave Evelyn alone for long.

She had been annoyed by his presence at first, afraid he might be itching to continue their disagreement or demand his apology. But instead, he simply acted as though nothing out of the ordinary happened at the event and they were still the best of workmates. Evelyn had been more than happy to go along with the façade. He asked her where she had run off to and she told him about the mysterious presence in the Sumerian wing.

"But if that were true," she said, "how did they escape so

fast? That is a long hallway. When I opened the door, I should have seen them still running away."

"Maybe they ducked down another hall or hid behind something," he said.

She sighed and shook her head. She knew it was silly to suggest the person—or naughty couple—had simply vanished, but she had explored the other options. But if she continued to press her case, she knew she would just appear mad.

"I suppose you are right," she said, turning back to her notes. "What brought you down to my lair anyway?"

"Oh," he said, as though he had forgotten. He reached into his coat's breast pocket and pulled out an envelope. "This came for you. Not sure why it was addressed to the museum."

She reached for it and read the front. In an ancient Greek script was written, *A curse upon any except Evelyn Crowley who attempts to read this missive.*

"Who...who delivered it?" she asked, her throat suddenly feeling parched.

"Just an errand boy," he said. "I tipped him and he ran off before I got a good look at him."

"Did you read it?" she asked.

"The front, of course," he said, clearing his throat. "But I didn't open it, if that's what you're asking."

Evelyn turned the envelope over and opened it. It was sealed, but it would have been no trouble for Henry to have re-sealed it from supplies in his own office upstairs. She had never suspected in the past that he would open something addressed to her, but she had never received something so cryptic before. And something in his voice led her to believe he wasn't being entirely honest.

When she opened it, though, she realized that if Henry

had opened the letter, he probably hadn't gotten much out of it. Like the script on the front, it was written in ancient Greek. Henry's modern Greek was passable enough, but his understanding of Attic or Koine was elementary at best. Still, she was sure to position herself and hold the letter as she read it to prevent him from trying to read over her shoulder.

Lady Sommers,

It has come to my attention that you are the preeminent translator of ancient languages, including Sumerian. I have in my possession an antique tome that I wish to know the contents of. I would like for you to come work for me at my estate. I trust no one else with this assignment. If you accept, a carriage will arrive at your home tomorrow at 9 a.m. Bring whatever you need for a stay of at least several weeks, including your maid. You will be handsomely compensated.

Sincerely,

Lord Craven

She felt a tightening in her chest. This was an incredible opportunity. A chance to work in a private setting with a patron was a translator's dream. And yet, she knew it must be too good to be true. Or even a cruel prank. After her run-in with Jane, she wouldn't put anything devious past her.

"The preeminent translator of ancient languages" indeed! She had never translated anything outside the museum, and she didn't even get credit for that. Henry did. She had never had any of her translations published. No one outside the museum community would know she knew anything of Sumerian. And even most of those who knew she was capable thought she was little more than a hobbyist.

No, she certainly was nowhere near the rank of preeminent translator. It had to be some sort of trick.

"Who is Lord Craven?" Evelyn asked Henry, who she just realized seemed to be waiting with baited breath for her to share the contents of the letter with him.

"Craven?" he asked. "You mean Bannister Shaw, Lord Craven?"

She only shrugged since she didn't know.

"Is that who sent you the letter?" he asked, but he didn't wait for her to confirm. "Eccentric old hermit. Haven't seen him in years."

"But who is he?" Evelyn pushed.

"He was a well-known adventurer in years past," Henry explained. "In *many* years past. He was one of the original museum directors. But once they started pooling their collections, he refused to contribute. He wanted to keep everything he found for himself."

Evelyn nodded for him to continue. She knew that joint excavation partnerships often dissolved in nasty ways over disagreements about how to divvy up the findings.

"He could have been one of the preeminent archeologists of our time, according to what the directors have told me," Henry went on. "But he just hoarded it all like a cursed dragon.

"Over the years, various museum members have gone to him, begging for him to donate at least some of his findings to the museum, but he always refused us."

"Us?" Evelyn asked.

"Oh yes," he said. "Even I went once, back when I was new here. I was eager to impress my new employers. Thought I could cement my position here quickly if I were able to get the old coot to release even one of his precious artifacts."

Evelyn snorted a laugh. "So cruel. You can't go around

insulting people for refusing to give you their prized possessions."

"Oh bah," Henry said, brushing her words away. "You haven't met him. And you don't have to worry about a job or keeping this place afloat."

"Hmm," Evelyn said, returning to her work. "Well, I suppose I'll form my own opinions soon enough."

"What the devil are you on about?" Henry asked. "You aren't going to meet him, are you?"

"It just so happens," she said, "that he's offered me a job, translating one of his precious Sumerian books."

"You must be joking," Henry said. "He's offered *you* a job? You? Why you?"

"Why not me?" she asked, holding up the letter. "He called me, 'the preeminent translator of ancient Sumerian.'"

"That's ridiculous," Henry said, reaching to snatch the letter away from her, but she jerked her hand back.

"How is it ridiculous?" Evelyn asked. "Do you know anyone who can translate Sumerian with even a fraction of my skill?"

"Me," Henry dared to say.

Evelyn barked a laugh, but then caught herself. "Now who is being ridiculous? We both know I'm infinitely better than you."

"But you and I are the only people who know that," Henry said, his voice bordering on a yell. "How did this man hear of you? Of your abilities? You surely cannot trust him."

"Why not?" Evelyn asked. "You said he could have been a great archeologist. He might be an eccentric hermit, but if his collection is anywhere near as incredible as you suggest, how can I refuse? Someone needs to get in there and see what he has."

"But not you," Henry said. "It's not proper. A lady holed up in a mansion with an old widower? It's not right."

Evelyn, in her annoyance, did see his point there. Such an arrangement would be improper. Even for her, a woman bordering on spinsterhood. The museum directors might even have to put her "volunteerism" to an end if she were a lady of poor reputation.

She turned back to her work. "I see," she said curtly. "Of course."

"You...see?" Henry said, as though he was surprised she had agreed with him.

Evelyn then uttered the words she knew he would be dying to hear. "You're right."

"I...am?" he asked. Then he smiled and his chest inflated. "I mean, yes, of course I'm right."

"Indeed," Evelyn said as she furiously scribbled her notes.

"So...we shall have no more talk of taking on this...position, or whatever?" he asked as he backed away slowly before she changed her mind.

"You and I will say nothing more about it," she said. She folded the letter up and stuffed it into her bag.

"Very good," Henry said. "Well, I'll just let you get back to your work then."

"Don't worry," she said, standing up from her stool and closing her notebook and bag. "I've just finished and...will you look at that?" She motioned to a grandfather clock near the door. "Just six o'clock. I'll be heading home."

"I'll walk with you," Henry said. "Have you seen the papers? All those missing girls? It's not safe for a proper young lady to be out alone."

Evelyn brushed past him and walked up the stairs. "Goodness. A proper lady can't be inside a house with a decrepit old man. We can't be out in public. Is there anywhere a woman can go nowadays?"

Henry walked ahead to open the museum's front door for her and chuckled. "The woman's place is in the home, as they say."

"Which is where I shall be headed then," she said. "Good night, Mr. Wilkes."

"If you just let me grab my hat and brolly, I'll—" Henry tried to say to get her to slow down, but Evelyn was already down the front steps.

"Oh, I couldn't dream of bothering you," she said. "I'm sure you still have so much work to do."

"It's no problem—"

"Goodnight, Mr. Wilkes," she said as she headed down the street without waiting to hear his further objections, the featherlight weight of the letter from Lord Craven pulling at her shoulder like a dog nipping at her heels.

CHAPTER FOUR

"*I* swear I never saw a more adorable creature!" Susan exclaimed as she prattled on about a cat she saw in a shop that day.

"You say that about every cat you see," Evelyn said as she sat in front of her vanity while Susan brushed out her long, thick hair. If nothing else, Evelyn had to have a maid just to help with the nightly ritual of combing through the incredibly thick locks and then plaiting the hair to keep it from tangling in the night.

"Oh, but this time it was true, I swear it!" Susan went on. "So fluffy with the most sparkling blue eyes. A more pleasant companion I'm sure you'd never find."

"Why don't you just get a cat of your own?" Evelyn said. "I wouldn't mind a kitchen mouser. You can keep it downstairs."

"I'm not sure about that," Susan said glumly. "I...Well, you know how it is. Things happen. Servants come and go. And if I had to leave your service, another mistress might not take kindly to me bringing a cat in."

Evelyn fidgeted with a brooch on her table as the two

went silent. She wasn't sure why this information—which was just a fact of life—made her feel ashamed, but it did. It wasn't right that someone like Evelyn should have every manner of security and stability while someone as hard-working as Susan should always have to worry about every aspect of the future. Even though Evelyn had no intention of letting Susan go, she couldn't predict the future. Should she have a sudden terrible accident—like her father did—Susan and the rest of the staff would find themselves out of work without a moment's notice. It had already happened in this house many times. After Evelyn's mother died, not only her maid but most of the household staff were dismissed. Evelyn was sent to Persia to live with her father, so there was no need to have staff in the London house. After Evelyn's father died, his valet was dismissed. Evelyn even now only kept what most families considered a skeleton of what a proper household should. She didn't even have a butler, only a footman who also answered the door on the rare occasion someone should call.

"I received the most odd letter today," Evelyn said, changing the subject.

"Oh?" Susan said as she tied the end of Evelyn's plait.

Evelyn stood up and walked over to her satchel, pulling out the letter. She knew Susan wouldn't be able to read it, but she would find it interesting nonetheless.

"Why is it written in code?" Susan asked.

Evelyn chuckled. "It's ancient Greek," she said. "I think Lord Craven wrote it that way so no one else could read it."

"Lord Craven?" Susan asked, a slight tremble in her voice. "I don't like the sound of that."

"Why not?" Evelyn asked. "Do you know him?"

"Only by reputation," Susan said, handing the letter back to Evelyn. "He is always advertising for staff, and pays well. But I've heard he's a right mean old man. Hit a maid with a cane once."

"That's dreadful," Evelyn said.

"Why is he writing to you?" Susan asked, gathering up Evelyn's clothes and sorting them to either be hung up or washed.

"He has a job for me," Evelyn said. "Translating an ancient text. He wants me to stay at his estate to complete the job...and bring my maid with me. For propriety's sake, I'm sure."

Susan looked up, her face blanched white. "You...Did you accept?"

"Not yet," Evelyn said, sitting on a bench at the end of her bed. "He's sending a carriage tomorrow. I'm to get in it if I want the job."

"Do you?" Susan asked.

Yes, Evelyn instinctively wanted to say. But she looked down at the letter and ran her fingers over the parchment. "Henry thinks I should decline."

Susan scoffed. "How you put up with that pompous poof day in and out I'll never understand."

"Pompous poof?" Evelyn asked, trying not to laugh.

"That was the nicest phrase that popped into my head," Susan said. "He doesn't respect you, ma'am. He wants to marry you, but only so you'll be his little wife who will occasionally translate things for him to make him look smart."

Evelyn sighed. "I know. But he's the only person who gives me access to any sort of job to use my skills at all. Even if I don't get any credit for my work, at least I'm able to use my mind instead of sitting at home reading to myself."

"And that's why you want to take this job?" Susan asked, much to Evelyn's surprise. "I can see it on your face that you want to accept. A real job, in your own right. Out of Henry's shadow."

"Something like that," Evelyn said, fighting back tears. The person who knew her best in the world was someone she could never truly count as a friend because they were separated by class. As usual, it wasn't fair.

"So why haven't you accepted?" Susan asked, sitting on the bench next to her.

"As you said, the man has an...unsavory reputation," Evelyn said. "And a woman staying in a house alone with a man—even one as old as Lord Craven—would be frowned upon. And there's you—"

"Me?" Susan asked, surprised. "What have I done?"

"Nothing," Evelyn said, patting Susan's hand. "But I would have to take my maid with me and I didn't know if you would be comfortable with that."

"I'd go wherever you need me to, m'lady," Susan said.

"But you just said how terrible Lord Craven was," Evelyn said.

"Oh posh," Susan replied. "Staying at his home as a guest is not the same as working for him. If you want to accept the job, then you should, and I'll happily go with you."

"Oh, I still don't know!" Evelyn said. "What will people think?"

Susan looked around. "What people?"

"You know...everyone. Society."

Susan pressed her lips to keep from saying what they were both thinking. Evelyn had not been part of "society" for years. She had no friends and no suitors. She couldn't think of one person who would actually care if she spent a few weeks in the home of an elderly lord.

Well, she could think of one person.

"And...Henry," Evelyn finally added.

Susan rolled her eyes. "If I never hear the name of that man again it would be too soon."

"But we have to consider him," Evelyn said. "Whether the job with Lord Craven works out for good or ill, the job will end. Then what will I do? If I want to go back to the museum, I'll need Henry's support."

"Maybe you won't have to go back to the museum," Susan said. "Lord Craven, if he is happy with your work, he could open more opportunities for you."

"You think so?" Evelyn asked.

"He's like your father, right?" Susan went on. "A treasure hunter. Those men always have more money than brains. He probably has lots of things for you to translate. Enough work for you to do until he dies. And all of his frumpy friends, they might have jobs for you too. They might want to take you back to Persia or Egypt and have you do work for them on the spot!"

Evelyn's heart began to race at the thought. Going back to the Near East or North Africa was her dream. How she missed it! The people. The history. The sand and sun. The fresh clean air. It was so unlike life here in London where there seemed to be a perpetual gloom and thickness to the air even on the clearest of days.

Unfortunately, it was nearly impossible and unheard of for a lady to travel such a distance and to such a place alone. She always imagined that she wouldn't be able to return until she found a husband willing to take her. But as she got older and the suitors never came, she feared she would be stuck in London for the rest of her life.

She had never considered being able to travel back to Persia with a patron or employer. Unfortunately, she didn't have any real credentials as a translator. Though she could certainly demonstrate her abilities if asked, she didn't have a degree or any publications or any sponsors behind her. Lord Craven's offer could change all that. She'd have job experience all her own, not one linked to or claimed by Henry Wilkes. Even if Lord Craven didn't have more jobs for her after she finished the book, surely he could give her a recommendation. She could then reach out to all the known treasure hunters among the upper class and find another patron.

Evelyn was so excited, she was nearly shaking as she stood and paced the room.

"Is...is this really happening?" she asked Susan. "Is it possible? Am I...Are *we* accepting the position?"

Susan smiled and walked over to Evelyn, squeezing her hand. "We are."

They both squealed in excitement.

CHAPTER FIVE

$\mathcal{T}$he next morning, Evelyn and Susan were ready and waiting when a large black coach pulled up outside their house at nine o'clock.

Actually, they had been ready and were waiting in the parlor for at least an hour by the time the coach arrived they were so excited. They had barely even slept the night before, but had been up until at least four o'clock packing everything they might need for an extended stay. Neither of them was tired, though. The adrenaline kept them alert.

As soon as the carriage pulled up, Susan opened the door and Evelyn stepped out. She looked up at the grey, overcast sky, a bit disappointed that such dreariness over-shadowed what she hoped was the start of the new life and a bright new future. But she had expected far too much from an English summer.

Still, she kept her head up as she carried her satchel and small personal bag down the front steps. The large black horses stomped their feet and let out what sounded more like growls than whinnies as she approached. The coach driver didn't leave his seat but turned his head slightly to look at her. His hat was so low and his collar so high she couldn't even see his face, but she gave an awkward nod all the same.

From the back of the coach, a tall footman descended, opening the door for her.

"M'lady," he said in a deep voice. She couldn't quite place an age on him, though he seemed a bit old to still be a footman. He was thin and lanky with thin black hair and an unsmiling face.

"My luggage," was all she could manage to say as she motioned back up the steps toward Susan, who was still waiting by the open door.

If it had not been impertinent, she would swear the footman suppressed a groan. He managed to constrain himself that much at least as he went up the steps without a word and picked up the trunk. Susan closed the door behind him and walked down the steps carrying her personal bag and another bag of Evelyn's personal items.

As the footman loaded the trunk, Evelyn did not wait for him to finish but helped herself and then Susan into the coach. The footman then closed the door behind him without a word and they felt the coach shift as he climbed up to his perch on the back.

"Cheery fellow," Susan mumbled, and Evelyn sighed her agreement. She had no idea why the men seemed so dower and worried they were a reflection of the lord they served.

The coach driver cracked his whip and the carriage lurched forward.

"We don't have to stay, you know," Susan said as they rode along through London's familiar streets.

"What do you mean?" Evelyn asked. "Have you changed your mind?"

"Not yet," Susan said. "But...we don't know what will happen when we get there. If you aren't comfortable or don't enjoy the work, we can always leave."

"I appreciate the sentiment," Evelyn said. "But we have to go into this with a positive attitude. Any difficulties will surely be easily overcome."

"My mum always said to hope for the best but plan for the worst," Susan said. "Always have an escape route."

"We must have her sew such a sentiment onto a pillow for me," Evelyn said with a smirk, which Susan returned.

Evelyn watched out the window as the scenery changed from the familiar, to the rarely visited, to the wholly new. They exited London by the east and traveled to an area she had never been before. It was very nearly like being in the countryside even though they hadn't really traveled very far. Rolling green hills and fields of sheep and cows stretched for miles. Finally, the coach turned down a lane and headed for Lord Craven's estate.

When she learned that Lord Craven had a London House, she imagined it was rather like hers—two stories and a basement with ten to twelve comfortable rooms. Instead, she sat in the carriage in awe at the sheer massiveness of a proper country estate. It had three main stories—not counting the basement—but was four stories tall on each corner and looked to be at least five stories tall in the back. Impressive spires shot up into the sky. It must have had hundreds of rooms.

"Oh...my word..." gasped Susan as the footman opened the door and helped the ladies step out onto the gravel driveway. "Lord Craven must have a hundred servants!"

Evelyn chuckled and wondered if Susan had never really seen a country house before. In truth, Susan wasn't far off. A house this size, if Lord Craven had a wife and children and hosted guests often, would need a veritable army to keep everything clean and orderly. However, since the man was now an old recluse, she suspected he had only a fraction of what he needed to keep the house from falling into disrepair.

The front door opened as Evelyn and Susan approached.

"Servants use the back entrance," an old woman said coldly as she eyed Susan.

"And you are?" Evelyn asked. She hadn't needed to be much of a commanding lady in her own home, but she didn't appreciate the woman giving orders to her maid.

"Mrs. Paxton," the woman said, folding her hands in front of her and looking down her nose at Evelyn. "The housekeeper."

"A pleasure to meet you, Mrs. Paxton," Evelyn said. "This is Susan, and she will help me bring in my things. I'm sure you wish for her to feel welcome. In the future, I am sure she would be happy to follow house protocol."

"Ma'am, I must insist—" Mrs. Paxton began, but Evelyn interrupted.

"I'm sure you do," she said. "But I've made my decision."

Mrs. Paxton and Evelyn stared at each other, neither budging. As far as Evelyn was aware, there was no lady of the manor, so Mrs. Paxton was probably used to being the highest-ranking woman she knew. Evelyn didn't like having to lord her position over people, but neither would she accept disrespect.

"This way," Mrs. Paxton finally said as she turned toward an impressive staircase behind her.

Evelyn heard Susan audibly exhale behind her, so she gave her a quick reassuring look.

As they followed Mrs. Paxton up the stairs, she couldn't help but notice that—as she suspected—the house was not in pristine condition. Most of the curtains weren't even open, so the house was quite dark. The rugs were dingy, as though they hadn't been taken out and beaten in years. The floors creaked and every surface seemed to be covered in a fine layer of dust. She didn't want to blame Mrs. Paxton for the home's poor condition—she doubted the woman had enough staff to keep up—but she was surprised she hadn't made more of an effort when she knew there would be guests.

"This will be your room," Mrs. Paxton said, stopping in front of a door on the second floor. "Will your maid be sleeping with you as well?"

Yes, Evelyn wanted to say. At the moment, she didn't want to let Susan out of her sight. And she certainly didn't want to leave her alone with this old battleax. But she held her tongue.

"Of course not," she said. "A room in the servants' quarters will be fine. After Susan has helped me unpack, you can show her to her own room."

"Very well," Mrs. Paxton said as she opened the door to the room. "I'm sure the footman will arrive with your trunk shortly. We serve luncheon at exactly noon. You'll meet Lord Craven then."

"Thank you," Evelyn said as she stepped into the room, Susan close behind her.

Mrs. Paxton then turned and left without any sort of by your leave.

"Well, I never," Susan gasped as soon as the old housekeeper was out of earshot. "If I ever grow that rude in my old age I hope you box my ears."

Evelyn laughed as she surveyed the room. "At least she seems to have given this room a proper going over before we arrived."

The room was as clean as she could have asked. Not a speck of dust was to be found on the furnishings or the mantle over the fireplace. Susan let out a sigh of relief when no moths flew from the armoire when she opened its doors.

Evelyn laid her bags on the bed and made her way to the window. She could see the brown, overgrown gardens below and then fields of green beyond.

"Such a shame," Susan said. "All seems to be going to waste."

"It is Lord Craven's house and money," Evelyn said. "We are not in a position to judge how he chooses to live."

They both gasped as they heard a heavy *thump!* outside the door.

"Must be the footman with the trunk," Evelyn said.

"Oh, of course," Susan said, but when she looked out into the hall, nothing—and no one—was there.

"Hello?" Susan called out. She retreated back into the room and closed the door. She then locked it for good measure.

"What are you doing?" Evelyn chuckled.

"These people and this place..." Susan said with a shudder. "It gives me the creeps. Are you sure you want to stay?"

"We are not going anywhere," Evelyn insisted. "But it might not go amiss to have you stay in my room."

Susan let out a huge sigh. "Oh, m'lady! You've made my heart right glad!"

"Come on, let's unpack," Evelyn said. "Then you can

help me dress for luncheon and to meet the Lord of the Manor."

*A*s the clock in Evelyn's room struck noon, Mrs. Paxton knocked at the door.

"Luncheon is served, m'lady," she said. "Susan will have her lunch in the kitchen with the rest of the staff."

"Of course," Evelyn said as she and Susan followed Mrs. Paxton down the stairs to the dining room. "My trunk never was delivered to my room."

"I'll see to it," Mrs. Paxton replied shortly. She led Evelyn to a door, but didn't open it. "This is the breakfast and luncheon room. Will you have breakfast here or in bed?"

"Where does Lord Craven have breakfast?" Evelyn asked.

"Here," Mrs. Paxton answered,

"Then I will eat here as well," Evelyn replied.

"Very well," Mrs. Paxton said. "Will you be able to find your way back to your room?"

No, she thought to herself as she looked around. "Of course," she said.

"Very well. Follow me, girl," Mrs. Paxton said to Susan as she turned away.

Girl? Susan mouthed to Evelyn as she walked past her to follow Mrs. Paxton.

Evelyn just shrugged and rolled her eyes. Perhaps she could speak to Lord Craven about Mrs. Paxton's treatment of Susan.

She faced the door and took a deep breath before turning the handle.

It was a good thing she did, because the young man standing there when she entered the room was so handsome he stole her breath away.

The man bowed. "Lady Sommers," he said. "You honor me with your presence."

"E-E-Evelyn," she stuttered. "Evelyn is fine. I haven't been called Lady Sommers in years."

The man smiled and nodded. "Of course, Evelyn."

Evelyn's stomach melted as her name slid off of his tongue. "Wh-wh-who are you?" she finally managed to spurt out.

"Forgive me," he said as he crossed the room and took her hand. "I am Lord Craven."

She looked at him and blinked several times. "You? I was told that Lord Craven was much older. One of the museum's original directors."

"That would be my father, Bannister Shaw," the man said. "I am Alister."

"It's a pleasure to meet you," she said and noticed that Alister was still holding her hand. He lifted her hand to his mouth and gently kissed the back of it. Shivers ran down her spine.

"Please," he said, releasing her hand and motioning toward the table. "Will you still join me? I will explain everything."

"Of course," she said. Alister pulled out her chair for her before settling into his own. A footman then proceeded to serve their luncheon and pour the wine.

"So, where is your father?" Evelyn asked.

"Dead, I'm afraid," Alister said, causing Evelyn to nearly spit her wine across the table.

"Dead?" she sputtered.

"He passed some weeks ago," Alister said.

"Weeks?" Evelyn asked. "Then who sent me the letter?"

"I did," he said.

"You? But...the Greek. It was flawless."

"This surprises you?" he asked.

Evelyn shook her head as she tried to make sense of it. "Well...yes. As I said, I was expecting an old world traveler and collector of antiquities. It would not surprise me if he could write archaic Greek so clearly. But I know nothing about you. I didn't even know Lord Craven had a son."

"You are a London lady," Alister said. "I am sure your command of Greek, Sumerian, and Arabic surprises all you meet."

"Indeed, it does," she said. "Forgive me, I think I am just in a bit of shock."

"Nothing to forgive," he said. "Perhaps I should explain. My father was, as you say, a traveler and collector. But he spent the last ten years cooped up here in this house. I do not know what happened to cause this. I was away at school for many years and then embarking upon my own travels. I only returned home a few days before his death when he sent for me telling me his time was near."

"I'm so sorry," Evelyn said.

"We were not close," Alister said matter-of-factly.

"Still," Evelyn said. "The loss of a parent is always difficult."

"Indeed," he said, still not conveying any more emotion over the loss of his father than if he had never met the man. "My father was a private man. I have not even made his death public except to my solicitor for fear people will use the opportunity to intrude upon this house and make inquiries about his expansive collection of items."

Evelyn nodded knowingly. She had a feeling that as soon as Henry Wilkes found out about the old lord's death, he would be the first person knocking at the door to pressure Alister into donating the collection.

"Unfortunately, the news will have to be made public eventually," Evelyn said.

"This is true," Alister said. "But I hope to have already decided what to do with my father's possessions by then. I will then sell this ridiculous house and resume my travels."

Evelyn felt her heart jump. She realized quickly she was having a pang of jealousy. How fortunate to be a man! He could simply leave all cares behind and travel anywhere in the world he wanted. To have such freedom of her own!

"That sounds wonderful," she said as she took another sip of her wine. "But what role do I play in all this?"

"Just as I said in my letter, I do have a book I wish you to translate," Alister explained. "It was my father's prized possession. He spent years puzzling over it, trying to understand the meaning. In his honor, I would like the book to be translated."

"I am honored to have been selected for the task," Evelyn said. "But how did you hear of me? I didn't think anyone outside the museum knew that I had an interest in Sumerian."

"An *interest*?" Alister said with a laugh. "My dear, are you truly this humble or only pretending? Do you think there is anyone else in London up to such a task? And do you really think such a talent is a secret?"

Evelyn blushed. Did she have more of a reputation than she realized?

"It would be nice if more people talked *to* me instead of just about me," she said, and not a little bitterly.

"Believe me," Alister said. "If you are able to translate this text for me, everyone in the world will want to talk to you."

Evelyn's heart raced. It seemed too good to be true. Would she really gain the reputation that would open the doors for her she had imagined?

"Well," she said, pushing her plate of barely touched food away from her. "Shall we get started?"

CHAPTER SIX

"How are you liking the house so far?" Alister asked Evelyn as they made their way toward the library.

"It's...big," Evelyn said. "Much larger than I expected."

"You've never been to a country estate before?" he asked, but not in a condescending way.

"I would visit with friends with Mother when I was little," Evelyn said. "But we didn't have one. Mama didn't see the point with just the two of us around. But when I heard that Lord Craven had a London house I imagined a townhouse. Not a proper estate."

"Actually, it's a castle," he said. "Carnarvon Castle. Named for the first Lord Craven—Carnarvon Shaw. It's the largest county estate in the area, certainly. Only Kensington and Buckingham are bigger, I believe."

Evelyn raised her eyes and took in the large chandelier hanging over the entryway, the spiderwebs dancing in the breeze.

"It must be difficult to keep up with," she said. "You seem quite understaffed."

"I'm inclined to agree," Alister said as they walked through room after room. "Though I don't really know what it takes to manage such a house. My mother died when I was young, so I've spent my life at boarding schools and then traveling."

Evelyn nodded. "My mother died when I was ten. Then I went to Egypt with my father. Then we went to Persia."

"Do you miss it?" Alister asked.

"Every day," Evelyn said quickly.

"Why don't you go back?" Alister asked.

Evelyn grimaced. She knew he was being polite, but did he really not know the barriers women faced when it came to being able to accept employment from an elderly man across town, much less traveling to the other side of the world.

"It's rather complicated," Evelyn said and left it at that.

Alister nodded. "Well, if there is anything you need, do let me know."

"Actually," Evelyn said. "I did have a request. It's rather unorthodox, I'm afraid."

"Name it!" Alister said, as though excited to get a chance to extend his hospitality further.

"As you said, the house is so huge," Evelyn said. "I...I'm almost embarrassed to say that I'm not used to having my maid so far away. Would it be possible to set her up in a room closer to mine? I know your housekeeper will probably frown on the idea of a maid staying in a guest room, but—"

"Don't let that old crone concern you," Alister said through gritted teeth. Evelyn paused at this sudden display of anger from the young lord. "Forgive me," he said, running his fingers through his dark hair. "Mrs. Paxton and I...do not see eye to eye."

"I can understand," Evelyn said, giving a small smile to lighten the mood. "The sudden death of her master and the arrival of a new one she barely knows. The changes must be hard on everyone."

Alister forced a smile to his face. "Quite," he said. "Do not worry. I'll make sure your maid is taken care of by this evening."

"Thank you," Evelyn said, feeling a little relieved. She wasn't the only one who found the housekeeper abrasive. It was good to know that Alister would support her should they continue to butt heads.

Alister finally stopped in front of a large set of double doors. "I don't mean to be dramatic..." he started to say.

Evelyn cocked an eyebrow at him in disbelief.

"Perhaps a little dramatic," he admitted. "But I want you to prepare yourself for what you are about to see—probably the greatest collection of the written word known to man."

Evelyn guffawed. "Such a claim! I've been to some of the largest libraries in Baghdad. You have a lot to live up to."

The smile fell from Alister's face for a moment. "I sometimes forget I am not in the presence of a typical London girl."

Evelyn shook her head. "Come now, you've piqued my interest! Open the door!"

Alister opened both doors at once, and Evelyn breezed into the room.

Alister had not been exaggerating. The room was huge. It must have taken up a quarter of the first floor. It looked as though the ceiling had at one point been removed, so the walls were double the height of the rest of the house. On one side of the room, large windows stretched from floor to ceiling. And everywhere there wasn't a window there was a wall lined with shelves of books.

Evelyn put her hands to her mouth as she gasped. The curtains were open, illuminating the room. A spiral staircase to one side led to a narrow galley around the room so people could reach the books on the higher levels. Still, there were small ladders throughout the room to make the books on the higher shelves accessible. The room also displayed various artifacts, such as statues and vases.

The library was not as large as some she had been to in Persia, or even Egypt, but it was larger than any she had ever seen in a private house in any country.

She chose a wall at random and looked at the titles. Books on law, mathematics, and science were all haphazardly thrown together in every language imaginable. She also found stacks of scrolls, Asian bamboo slips, and cuneiform tablets!

"This collection..." Evelyn shook her head, wondering if Alister knew the true value of what this room contained.

Alister sighed. "Yes, I know. For a world traveler such as yourself, it must be quite pitiful."

"No," she said breathlessly. "It's magnificent! I've never seen the like here in London, not even at the museum. No wonder people so want to get their hands on it. You simply must hire an archivist to catalog everything before you decide what to do with your father's estate."

"Oh," he said, somewhat dejected sounding. "I had no idea it would be so complicated. Couldn't you do it?"

"Me?" she asked with a laugh, and then realized he was serious. "Oh, certainly not. This is a specialized sort of job. I'm a polyglot not a bean counter. But I can help you find someone. And I could assist whomever you hire if you wish."

Alister sighed in annoyance at the magnitude of the job. "Well, I suppose we can worry about that later. I'm sure you are anxious to see the book I actually brought you here to work on."

"Oh! Of course," Evelyn said. She had become so distracted by the treasure trove of books she forgot she had been brought here for one book in particular. Any one of these books probably contained information worthy of translation.

Alister walked over to a large wooden desk in the back of the room. Open upon it was a thick tome with a leather-bound cover and papyrus pages.

Her breath nearly went out of her when she saw it. There was something familiar about it, but she couldn't remember where she had seen it before. She ran her fingers over the papyrus and sighed as she looked at the unfamiliar characters.

"This...this isn't ancient Sumerian," she said.

"What?" Alister said, looking at the book as if he could make sense of it. "But my father said it was from Persia, from the Sumerian era."

"I mean..." Evelyn tried to find the words to explain the situation to him. "This is much older than the ancient Sumerian I can read, high Sumerian. This is...archaic Sumerian at best."

"What does that mean?" Alister asked.

"It's practically another language," Evelyn said. "Like someone who only speaks English trying to read Latin. One is based on the other and there are links and similarities, but trying to actually make sense of it..." Evelyn shook her head.

"Are you saying you can't translate it?" Alister asked, but she could not pinpoint his tone. Disappointment? Anger? Despair? He was good at masking his emotions.

"That's not…" She sighed and looked back at the book. "I just need a moment."

"Take all the time you need," he said, stepping away and looking out one of the windows, giving her space to work without him looking over her shoulder.

She sat down in the large leather chair that accompanied the desk and turned the pages of the book. She rubbed her fingers together, feeling a fine grit on them. The book was beyond old—it was ancient. She feared it would crumble under even her delicate touch. She would need some gloves if she planned to continue working with this book.

The book was more than just writing. Illustrations also covered many of the pages. Images of people and items. Flames and animals. People worshiping and hunting. Some of the images she had seen before, in carved reliefs or in other Sumerian books. Others were completely new to her. Whatever information the book contained, she was sure it would reveal much new information about ancient Sumerian culture. She wondered where old Lord Craven had gotten it and if the Persians knew he had taken it. Surely such an item would be of great value to the Sumerian descendants.

Even though she worked in a museum and her father had been a treasure hunter, Evelyn hated the idea that so many incredible items had been stolen from their homelands. While she believed that lost relics such as this book should be excavated, she also believed they should be left in their native lands. How would the English feel if foreigners came to London, dug up the tombs of the kings and queens at Westminster, and then carted the treasures and even the bodies off to the Near East? She didn't imagine people like her father or old Lord Craven would appreciate it one bit.

"Have you discovered anything?" Alister asked, interrupting her thoughts.

"The truth is, sir," she said, "that I cannot at this moment read this book."

Alister let out a long sigh laced with disappointment. "You cannot translate it."

"That's not what I said," she clarified. "Translating this book would be like an Englishman translating Latin without a primer. To steal an analogy from my maid, I need to decipher the code first."

"How can you do that?" Alister asked.

"There are similarities," she said. "See this character here? In high Sumerian, it represents life. And this one, death."

"And that is enough for you to go on?" he asked.

Evelyn slowly nodded. "It's a start. I can't make any promises. I have no idea how long it will take me to figure the writing system out or to make any sense of it once I do. I'll be translating one extinct language into another one and then into English. It is...a daunting task, to say the least."

"Are you willing to do it?" Alister asked. "I am sure that when you came here, you did not expect such a complicated job."

"I knew it wouldn't be easy," she said. "But I would at least like to try, if you will permit me. I know you probably thought I would be able to translate it more easily than this. I can't tell you how long it will take. Months...Years?"

"Years?" he exclaimed, taken aback.

"I'm sorry," she said. "It might not take that long. But I need you to be prepared. To understand the enormity of the task ahead. Are you sure that you want to dedicate so much of your life—of my life—to this? Is the book worth it to you?"

Alister wandered back to the window, seriously pondering the question she had put before him. In truth, she needed to put the question to herself as well. She had planned on spending a few weeks on the project and then figuring out the rest of her life. Could she really spend years working on translating one book?

As she looked back at the book and ran her fingers over it, she knew the answer was yes. The book called to her. She needed to know what it contained within its pages.

"Do it," Alister finally said, sending Evelyn's heart into a flurry. "However long it takes. Whatever you want to charge me for the work, money is no object."

"Your dedication to your father and to the study of Sumerian is admirable," she said, unable to contain her smile. Her excitement at taking on the task was threatening to bubble over.

He smiled back, his chest puffing up. "Anything you need, you have only to ask. And if there is any way I could help you—"

"Help me?" she asked. "Have you studied Sumerian?"

He blushed and looked away. "Umm...no."

"Forgive me," Evelyn said. "That sounded terribly snobbish of me. I only meant that your command of ancient Greek was so flawless, I thought maybe you had studied Sumerian as well."

"Unfortunately, my education was limited to more classical languages," Alister said. "Greek and Latin. Though I've been told I can converse in Italian like a native."

"You speak Italian?" Evelyn asked.

"Don't you?" Alister asked.

Evelyn shook her head. "Nor French, I'm afraid. Most people who speak the languages I know are dead. Except for Arabic."

"A lady who doesn't speak French?" Alister marveled. "Perhaps I will have something to teach you after all."

Evelyn felt a tingling low in her stomach. "Perhaps you will," she nearly whispered.

They stared at each other for a moment too long, grinning like fools. Alister finally broke away first.

"Well, I will let you get to it then," he said, crossing the room. "I'll find your maid, have her prepare your tea just the way you like it."

"That sounds wonderful," she said.

"And I'll see you at dinner tonight," he said as he opened the door.

"That sounds wonderful," she repeated, her mastery over words seeming to have fled her.

He chuckled and shut the door behind him.

She cursed herself for feeling so flustered. Like a foolish schoolgirl with a crush. Not that she had ever been a foolish school girl with a crush. But she couldn't deny that Alister Shaw was one of the most companionable men she had ever met. Handsome. Charming. And he spoke several languages and loved to travel. She wondered for a moment why he wasn't already married.

Bah. A man like that certainly wouldn't be interested in her. A strange girl who spent all her time in books and probably carried some sort of family curse. Besides, she needed to focus on her work.

She went and sat down back at the desk and turned to the front page of the book. Her heart stopped when she saw a character she knew all too well— *Utuk xul.*

Evil.

CHAPTER SEVEN

The task ahead of Evelyn was far more complicated than she had originally anticipated, so she hadn't brought all the supplies she would need for the job. She also hadn't told Henry that she wouldn't be returning to the museum any time soon.

She supposed there was a possibility she couldn't have accepted the job. She really hadn't known what she was walking into. If she'd needed to turn the job down for whatever reason, she could have simply returned to her home and to her volunteer position at the museum and Henry would have been none the wiser. No sense in worrying him unnecessarily. But since she had accepted the job—and it had proven to be a monumental task—she could not delay in informing him any further. She had already not shown up on Monday. If she failed to show on Tuesday, he would be in a complete tizzy. He might be already.

She had a note sent to him by messenger so it would arrive just before he left the museum on Monday evening. She expected a courier to arrive with her things at some point on Tuesday.

However, she had been in the library not more than a few minutes when Mrs. Paxton gave only a cursory knock at the door before letting herself in.

"A Mr. Wilkes to see you, ma'am," she announced, then promptly turned to leave.

"What?" Evelyn asked. "Here?"

"Are you somewhere else?" Mrs. Paxton asked.

Evelyn sighed and followed her out of the room. "I mean where in the house is he?"

"The front parlor," Mrs. Paxton offered, which didn't tell Evelyn much. The house was still a veritable labyrinth. Though she was glad Mrs. Paxton didn't show him to the library. She preferred to keep that to herself for now.

"Thank you," Evelyn said. "Please send up some tea."

"Hmm," Mrs. Paxton said through pressed lips as she slipped through a side door down to the kitchen.

Evelyn walked toward the front of the house, checking behind every door until she heard Henry's voice.

"I demand to see her now," he said.

"If you will give me her items," Susan said, "I'll see if she's available."

"Where is she?" Henry nearly yelled.

"What is the meaning of this?" Evelyn asked as she entered the room.

"I'm so sorry, m'lady," Susan said. "I didn't mean to disturb your work."

"You are not at fault," Evelyn said. "You would think Mr. Wilkes had never visited a proper house before."

"Evelyn," Henry said breathlessly as he crossed the room over to her. "I've been worried sick!"

Evelyn looked down and noticed he was carrying a small satchel. "Are those the things I asked for? The books and gloves?"

"What?" Henry asked as though he had forgotten he was even holding them until he looked at his hand. "Oh, yes. I brought them."

"Thank you," she said. "Susan, please take this to my room."

"Yes, miss," Susan said, retrieving the bag from Henry. She then left the room and mostly closed the door, but left it open a crack.

"Evelyn," Henry said. "What is going on? I thought you weren't going to accept the job."

"I had considered turning the offer down," Evelyn said, stepping away to put more space between them. "But Lord Craven was...quite persuasive."

"Where is the old goat?" Henry asked. "I'll give him a piece of my mind, putting you in this position—"

"What position?" Evelyn asked. "It's a good opportunity for me. A chance to make a name for myself."

"Make a name for yourself?" Henry asked. "Is that what this is about? Being famous? What do you want, a wing of the museum named after you?"

"No," Evelyn said. "But a proper job title wouldn't go amiss."

Henry laughed. "You are being ridiculous. You are a lady! You shouldn't be working at all. Now, come on. Collect your things. I'll take you home."

"What?" Evelyn asked. "I'm not leaving. I have a job to do. One that you are distracting me from, so I'm going to have to say good day to you."

"Evelyn," Henry said, lowering his voice and his gaze.

"What's going on?" Alister asked, stepping into the room.

Henry turned toward Alister, his eyes wide. "Who the devil are you?"

"Alister Shaw," Alister said. "Lord Craven, Bannister Shaw's son. But since you are in my house I think I should be asking who *you* are, *sir*."

"Alister," Evelyn stepped in. "This is Mr. Henry Wilkes. We worked together at the British Museum."

"Oh, of course," Alister said, offering Henry his hand and a polite smile. "I've heard so much about you. Curator for the Near East and North African collections, right?"

Henry seemed to stumble over his words, surprised that Alister knew who he was and was being so polite.

"Yes, sir," Henry said.

"So, what brings you here today?" Alister asked.

Henry started to speak, but Evelyn cut him off.

"I needed some translation materials from the museum," she said. "He was kind enough to bring them to me."

"And to check on your well-being," Henry added to Evelyn.

"Oh dear," Alister said. "Is something amiss with your well-being, Evelyn?"

"No," she said. "I'm perfectly fine."

"Come now," Henry said. "Mr. Shaw, surely you can see how unacceptable this situation is."

"In what way?" Alister asked innocently.

"A proper, unmarried lady cannot possibly be the guest in the home of an unmarried man—and his son—and there not be questions about her character," Henry said bluntly.

"Watch yourself, man," Alister said darkly. "You would dare speak ill of the character of this perfectly respectable young woman?"

"It is not the young woman I am worried about," Henry said.

Something seemed to snap inside Alister, for he nearly

growled as he grabbed Henry by the collar. "You dare to impugn my honor? In my own home?"

Henry gasped and stumbled over his words as he reached for Alister's wrists.

"Alister!" Evelyn cried, grabbing one of his arms. "I'm sure Henry meant no such insult. Did you, Henry?"

"Of course not," Henry finally said. Alister released Henry and then straightened the cuffs of his sleeves.

"Forgive me," Alister said. "That was most unbecoming of me."

"Please, Alister," Evelyn said with pleading eyes. "Perhaps go check on the tea I requested earlier of Mrs. Paxton?"

Alister ran his fingers through his hair and then nodded at Evelyn. "Do excuse me," he said to Henry. He didn't wait for a reply before leaving the room.

"That man—" Henry started to say, but Evelyn cut him off.

"You were out of line," Evelyn said. "Do you really think so low of me?"

"No," Henry said, as though he were the one insulted. "I think the world of you. But if I had known that not only would you be alone in this house with an elderly man but his much younger son, I never would have allowed you to take this position."

"*Allowed* me?" Evelyn asked. "Oh, Henry, do stop this nonsense. I'm not your concern. I have no father or brother to tell me what to do. I make my own decisions."

"Which is why you need a husband," Henry said. "You can't be burdened with having to take on such concerns yourself."

"I certainly do not need a husband," Evelyn said. "I have a good position here doing a job I am excited to take on. I appreciate all you have done for me in allowing me to work at the museum, but it is time I move on."

"But what will people think?" Henry asked.

"What people?" Evelyn asked. "I'm shunned by society. You saw the way Jane Poole treated me the other night."

"Jane Poole is a snob," Henry said. "Everyone knows that."

"You don't know her," Evelyn said. "You aren't a peer."

"I know people like her," Henry said. "All these frumped up lords and ladies, thinking they are better than the rest of us."

Evelyn raised an eyebrow and waited for him to realize who he was talking to.

"Not you," Henry corrected. "You aren't like the rest of them."

"Exactly," Evelyn said. "For once in my life being a social outcast is playing in my favor. No one will care that I've accepted this position. And it might open more doors for me later."

"Open doors where?" Henry asked. "What about the museum?"

"I...I don't think I'm returning to the museum," Evelyn finally said.

Henry stumbled back as though he had been wounded.

"I'm sorry," Evelyn said. "But I believe this job will take much longer than I thought. Months, or even years."

"Years?" Henry asked. "Have you lost your mind? What about marriage? Children?"

Evelyn blushed. "Those things aren't in the equation for me right now. I'm choosing to focus on this."

"Oh, Evelyn," Henry said, gripping her hand. "Don't say it. Don't give up on us. On what we could have. I know I'm not a peer like you, but I don't think you care about things like that. Forget this ridiculous job. Come back with me right now and we will say no more about it."

Evelyn felt her ears redden with anger, but she refused to lash out. She knew that Henry had developed feelings for her, but she had never been more than a friend and workmate to him. She felt nothing for him, other than the occasional disdain or annoyance when he didn't give her proper credit for her work. In truth, she didn't like him a jot. She only put up with him because he was the only person in the whole city willing to give her a job.

Until she met Alister Shaw.

She didn't have any reason to think that she and Alister would ever be more than friends or workmates, but at least he respected her expertise. He would never try to diminish her accomplishments or try to take credit for them himself. If she had to choose between being friends with Henry or being friends with Alister, Alister won by leaps and bounds.

"I'm sorry," Evelyn said kindly, removing her hand from Henry's. "But I'm staying here. I think you should leave."

Henry took a few deep breaths, his face reddening in anger. Evelyn was afraid for a moment he might lash out, but finally he simply turned on his heels and stormed out of the parlor.

Evelyn followed him into the entryway where he grabbed his hat and walking stick.

"You are going to regret this, Evelyn Crowley," Henry said.

"Henry," Evelyn said, exasperated. "There is no need to leave angry."

"Oh, there is every need," he said, opening the front day. "Good day to you, madam." Then he slammed the door.

Evelyn shook her head.

"Oh dear," said Alister walking up behind her. She

turned to see he was carrying a tea tray. "Has our guest left?"

"Fortunately, yes," Evelyn said.

"And here I am with all these refreshments," he said with a shrug.

"Well, we can't let them go to waste," Evelyn said, motioning for him to continue on into the parlor. She followed him into the room, where he placed the tray on a low table between two sofas.

"I do hope Mr. Wilkes didn't say anything else untoward after I left," Alister said.

"I'm sure he did," Evelyn said. "But I stopped listening after a while." Alister chuckled. "I did want to thank you, though."

"For what?" Alister asked. "Nearly punching him in the throat?"

"No," she said as she poured herself a cup of tea. "For walking away. For letting me speak for myself."

"Well, he is your acquaintance, not mine," Alister said.

The differences between Alister and Henry continued to mount. And for the first time in many years, Evelyn was enjoying some male company.

CHAPTER EIGHT

*E*velyn leaned back in her chair and looked up at the ceiling as she stretched her arms and her neck. She looked at the clock. It was nearly ten o'clock at night. She had completely lost track of time, but that had become the norm over the last week. She was completely engrossed in the work from morning until night. It was fascinating! While there were connections to the high Sumerian she was versed in, it was clear that syntax here was completely different. The way these people expressed themselves was unique from anything else she had ever studied. She wished she knew how a native speaker would have sounded. It must have been musical.

She enjoyed working uninterrupted and not having to worry about leaving her work at exactly six in the evening and being prevented from working on the weekends. She was only forced to stop working when Susan or Mrs. Paxton announce luncheon or supper. She would probably starve to death if people didn't remind her to take a break to eat.

Not that the meal breaks were unpleasant. Alister took most meals with her, unless he was out...doing whatever it is that young lords do. Probably chasing available young ladies and betting on horses. No, she had no reason to think that Alister was as frivolous as she imagined. She had only known him to be kind, courteous, and thoughtful. She really had no idea how he filled his time when he wasn't playing host to her. She hadn't asked as it wasn't her business.

Often after dinner and conversation, Alister would turn to a book and cigar in the smoking room and Evelyn would return to her work, hoping to get a bit more done before Susan finally dragged her off to bed. But even in her sleep, she dreamed of the book. In the mornings, she often awoke refreshed and excited as soon as the first rays of dawn filtered through the window, anxious to get started. She thought her mind often worked out little knotty problems in her sleep and wanted to jot down any new revelations before she forgot them. She could typically get an hour or two of work done even before breakfast.

She enjoyed what she was doing, but she wasn't sure how much headway she was really making. She had very little idea what the book was about. Evil was a word she saw frequently. As were ruler, life, and death. But that was hardly anything to go on. The Christian Bible and *Beowulf* also spoke of such things. Right now, she was mostly categorizing the characters and character groups, looking for similarities and patterns. It was a tedious but important part of the process.

She stood and walked over to the window. It was late at night, so it was hard to see much beyond her own reflection. But slowly, her eyes adjusted, and she thought she saw a faint red light slowly start to illuminate from behind a distant hill. She rubbed her eyes and nearly pressed her nose to the glass to get a better look. Was the light...pulsing? What was that?

She gasped in surprised when the door to the room opened.

"Alister!" she said as he entered the room.

He looked at her, confused. "I'm sorry. I didn't mean to startle you."

She turned back to the window. "I was just looking at...Huh."

Alister stepped up next to her. "Looking at what?"

"I thought I saw something," she said. "A strange light. But I think my eyes must be playing tricks on me." She chuckled in embarrassment.

Alister smiled. "Maybe your eyes are trying to tell you it is time to rest for the evening."

"Probably," she said, walking back over to the book and straightening her papers. "I'm afraid my body tires long before my mind does."

"Well, I think I may have something to show you that will send your mind whirling," Alister said.

"Oh?" Evelyn asked.

Alister gave a sneaky grin and held his hand out to her as if he was just about to escort her into a fancy ball. She placed her hand in his, feeling a warmth at their touch rush through her body.

He led her out of the room.

"You have been so busy," he said, "I forgot to give you a full tour of the house."

"Goodness," Evelyn said. "A tour of every room would take ages."

"Indeed," Alister said. "I don't think even I have been in every room. But there are a few I know you will enjoy."

"More libraries?" she asked as they climbed the stairs to

the second, and then the third floor. She was nearly winded as they reached the top. She couldn't imagine what the poor servants must go through every day, having to rush to and from their rooms on the fourth and fifth floors to the kitchen and their dining and socializing rooms in the basement.

Alister laughed. "Thankfully, no more libraries, but something I think you will find just as interesting."

They headed to the east wing, an area that clearly had not been used for living in for probably decades. The wallpaper was peeling, the carpeting worn through, and Evelyn was certain she saw a rat scurry by.

"I've been sorting through my father's collections," he said. "It has been a daunting task. And I think you are right that I will need to hire someone—or several someones— soon to assist me. But in the meantime, I have at least been trying to group things together by era or country of origin."

"If any of the items have any sort of documentation with them, be sure to keep it together," Evelyn said. "Any information can be useful for identification later."

"I've been doing my best," he said. "You wouldn't know it by the shape of this house, but I'm a stickler for organization. The haphazard way things are strewn about here has been driving me mad."

He opened a door and flicked on a light switch. "For example, this is where I have been putting things that are from ancient Egypt."

"Oh my word," Evelyn said as she put her hand to her mouth. She couldn't believe what she was looking at. With just a cursory glance around the room, she knew this collection was far more valuable than anything in the boxes from Lord Wenham she had just unpacked last week at the museum.

Statues of Bast and Anubis, canopic jars, staves and swords, and boxes of coins and jewelry were simply lying about. And across the room, standing in a corner, was a still wrapped mummy.

"This is unbelievable!" Evelyn said. Then she pointed to the mummy. "That needs to be given a more respectable resting place right away!"

Alister laughed. "There's more where that came from."

"Are you serious?" she asked.

"Oh yes," he said. "I found three more I haven't had the chance to move here yet."

Evelyn shook her head. The avarice of treasure hunters knew no bounds. What use was a mummy to anyone except the dead person's descendants? Yet she knew not only treasure hunters, but museums, and even anyone with a little money were obsessed with having mummies of their own. She had even heard of several members of the aristocracy hosting "unwrapping" parties, where the central feature of the gathering was to watch a mummy unwrapped as though the guests were watching a play. It was disgusting. Such events made Evelyn glad she wasn't friendly enough with anyone to ever be invited.

"Come," Alister said. "There's much more."

Evelyn shook her head as they left the room.

"The next one is, unfortunately, grouped by continent instead of country since I can't tell one from another," Alister said. "I give you Africa."

It appeared as though old Lord Craven was a trophy hunter as well. A stuffed lion and elephant greeted Evelyn as she entered the room. There were also tribal masks, ceremonial drums, and a large statue of a fertility goddess with overaccentuated breasts and buttocks.

"Are those..." Evelyn started to ask as she pointed to a collection of items hanging from leather cords.

"Shrunken heads?" Alister asked. "I do believe so."

"I can see why Henry Wilkes is so enchanted with the idea of having access to this collection," Evelyn said. "The museum would benefit greatly from having such displays. People would be lining the block for a glimpse."

"What do you think?" Alister asked. "Do you think all these items belong in a museum?"

Evelyn thought for a moment and tried to read his face before responding. Did he really want to know what she thought?

"I think it is incredible for people to be able to learn about other cultures they may not ever be able to travel to," she couched. Alister nodded, but waited for her to continue. "But we don't own them. They belong with their people. Unless the local people and governments give permission for the items to travel abroad, we shouldn't just take them. I believe that here in England, we would call such actions stealing."

"I'd ship the whole lot back if I could," Alister said. Evelyn thought she picked up disdain in his voice. It was clear that the man did not have a good reputation with his father. "It doesn't mean anything to me."

"Then why go to such lengths to translate the book?" Evelyn asked. "I mean, I'm grateful for the chance to study it. But if you don't care about your father's collection, why bother?"

Alister shrugged. "You know what is really tragic about all this?" He motioned around the room at the artifacts. "I don't think he gave a damn about this stuff either. He took it because he could. He didn't care about history or archeology or...anthro...whatever."

"Anthropology," Evelyn offered.

"Yes, anthropology," Alister said. "Other cultures and peoples. He just took it because he could. Then he kept it to himself because he could. He loved that the other museum directors wanted this junk."

Evelyn wanted to tell him that it wasn't junk to the people of Africa, but she held her tongue.

"The book was the only thing I think he truly cared about," Alister said. "And I aim to know why."

Evelyn nodded. "Then I will do what I can to help you," she said. "And then—together—we can figure out what to do with everything else."

"I look forward to it," Alister said, the smile returning to his face. "Almost as much as I look forward to seeing your face when I show you the next room."

"There's more?" she asked, following him back into the hallway.

"I saved the best for last," he said, opening the final door.

Her heart soared when she realized the room was full of Sumerian artifacts.

"Oh, Alister!" she exclaimed as she ran to a relief that depicted a king sitting on a throne accepting dignitaries from Africa who were presenting him with a cheetah. Next to that was a statue of a Sumerian Queen. Her large eyes and high cheekbones depicted a woman of great beauty. And on a nearby shelf were dozens of scrolls.

"Do you like it?" he asked.

"I can't believe you were keeping all this from me!" she said playfully. "They are exquisite."

He pulled out one of the scrolls and handed it to her. "Can you read it to me?"

Evelyn opened it up and was glad to see it was written in

high Sumerian. "Ten bushels of grain sell for ten sheckles," she read. "While twenty bushels shall be sold for not more than two denari."

"Are you toying with me?" he asked, pulling the scroll out of her hand and looking at it as though he could make sense of it on his own.

"I wish I were," she said. "But it seems to just be a report on market values at the time. It is still valuable, telling us what average life was like at the time, but I'm not sure it makes for very riveting reading."

"Well that's disappointing," Alister said, depositing the scroll back on the shelf with the others.

"No," Evelyn said. "It's wonderful! Thank you for showing me. I'm sure I will sneak up here anytime I need a break from the book."

"I'm glad you like it," Alister said as he looked down at her, the smile having fled from his face and his eyes burning into hers with what she could only identify as desire.

Her mouth went dry and she forced herself to look away. She couldn't give in. It was bad enough that they were living in the same house. If they did start to have feelings for each other—and dare to act on them—and anyone found out, she would be ruined. No. She was here to do a job. She had to be professional. After the work was done and she returned to her own house, if Alister decided to court her properly, then she could give into her growing feelings.

She cleared her throat and walked across the room to look at a gold bracelet that was sitting on a crate. "So, do you know anything about these items? When your father procured them? It could help to identify them."

Alister licked his lips and walked to the other side of the room, but he didn't seem to be looking at anything in particular. "From his last trip, I think," he said. "Before he became a recluse. About ten years ago, I suppose."

"Ten years ago?" Evelyn asked. "Are you sure?"

Alister nodded.

"Was he part of the Duncan Expedition?" she asked, her heart starting to race. "The one Lord Duncan sponsored. The one...the catastrophe?"

"No," Alister said. "I mean, how could he have been? He only just died..." Then he paused and put his hand to his mouth. "I'm sorry. I had forgotten about your father."

"You have no need to apologize," Evelyn said. "I just find it odd that your father was there at the same time. Are you sure?" She racked her brain, trying to remember. Had there been a Lord Craven there that day? She couldn't remember. She had forgotten so much about that day. Trapped in the sand, she had nearly died. Hamid...

"I'm sure he was there around the same time," Alister said. "But he must have been with another group. Or maybe he had left early."

Evelyn shook her head. Something wasn't right. She was suddenly so thirsty.

"Yes, I'm sure that's it," she said as she headed toward the door. "It's awfully late. We should probably call it a night."

"Of course," Alister said as he followed her out the door, but as he shut it, she was already halfway down the hall. "Shall I walk you to your room?" he called after her.

"No, I know the way," she called back. She just needed to get away from that room. Away from the memories threatening to burst forth. Away from the pain.

CHAPTER NINE

*E*velyn tossed and turned all night, barely getting a wink of sleep. Something was bothering her, deep in the back of her mind. It was as though the lost memories of the day her father died were seeping to the surface. But every time she tried to look more closely, the memories vanished again.

The next morning, she woke up before Susan, as usual. But instead of heading to the library to work, she went to the stables and asked the groom to prepare the coach to take her home.

"Are you leaving, miss?" the groom asked her.

"No," she explained. "I just need to find something."

"If you just need something picked up, I can fetch it for you," the groom helpfully offered. But Evelyn shook her head.

"Unfortunately, I'm not sure where it is," she said. "But it shouldn't take me long to find."

"Of course, miss," the groom said with a bow as he went to prepare the carriage with no more questions.

She wondered what Alister would think when she

didn't come down for breakfast. He would surely send Mrs. Paxton to check on her. And when she announced that Evelyn was gone, what would he think then? She should have left a note. But she wasn't sure what to say. She knew she had acted strangely last night. The whole incident had left her shaken. She had to find answers. And she hoped she knew where to find them. Once she did, she could return to Alistair's mansion and resume her work. There was no sense in alarming Alister about her sudden trip. He might try to dissuade her from leaving or, worse, want to accompany her. But she needed to do this on her own.

"M'lady!" her cook exclaimed when she opened the door. "What are you doing here? Is everything all right? Where is Susan?"

"Everything is fine," Evelyn said, handing the cook her hat. "I'm sorry for dropping by so suddenly."

"Forgive me, ma'am," the cook said. "It's your house. I was just surprised is all."

"I understand," Evelyn said as she started ascending the stairs. "I just need to find something."

"Shall I fix you some tea?" the cook asked.

"Hopefully I won't be here long enough," Evelyn called over the railing as she ascended from the second floor to the third.

Evelyn often forgot the house even had a third floor. It was mainly used for storage, housing old family heirlooms and her father's artifacts she hadn't been able to part with.

She went to a room at the end of the hallway and steeled herself before entering. She took a calming breath as she opened the door.

The room was not unlike the room of Sumerian artifacts in Alister's house. Even though Evelyn loved Persia and

Sumerian treasures, the items in this room all came from her father's last trip.

They had been in Persia for months, so every few weeks, her father would have the items he had collected or bought packaged and sent back home. They were all stored in this room, awaiting their master's return to decide what to do with them. Even though Evelyn had sorted through half a dozen other rooms of items, even many from Persia, sorting through the items in this room had seemed...too final. As though emptying this room would have been a last goodbye to her father she wasn't quite ready for.

But she wasn't here to examine old parchments, statues, or jewels. She was looking for something more mundane— the official documents from the trip. For some reason, she had a feeling old Lord Craven had been on that final trip with her father. She wasn't sure why this information mattered to her, but it did. It was as though Lord Craven was a missing piece to a puzzle she hadn't quite been able to complete.

In the back of the room, sitting on a desk, was the card-board box she sought. She threw open the curtains to let in enough light for her to see and stared at the box, hesitating to open it. She wasn't sure why. Did she want to open it or not? Why did it matter? What would it change? She wasn't sure, but she needed to find out.

She threw open the box lid and felt her heart still when she saw a photograph lying there. She took it out, running her fingers over the familiar faces. There she was, thirteen years old. A slip of a thing with her long black hair plaited over her shoulder. She was wearing a khaki-colored dress that buttoned down the front and bulky brown boots. Clothes more appropriate for desert adventuring than she ever could have gotten away with wearing here in England. She realized then how grateful she was that her father decided to take her with him after her mother died instead of sending her away to a boarding school as Alister's father had done with him. She scanned the image, reciting the names of each of the lords. She recognized and could name every one of them. There was no Lord Craven. There were several more people in the photograph, the local laborers, translators, and government officials. Her friend Hamid was there, standing to one side, his arms crossed. As was Hamid's father. Her father, all the other lords, Hamid and his father, and countless other Persians had died in the sandstorm that day. Evelyn nearly did as well.

In the sandpit under the tarp, Evelyn and the other survivors were trapped for days. The sand that had been blown over the tarp had been too heavy for them to crawl out of. They had quickly run out of water and food, and were on their way to running out of air. They couldn't light a torch because the fire would have devoured the oxygen too quickly. So they sat in the dark and waited for a slow death to claim them. Even now, just thinking about that time made Evelyn's throat parch.

Evelyn sighed and shook her head, laying the picture aside. This was probably a mistake. What good was going to come from digging up these old painful memories?

She then pulled out a newspaper clipping about the incident. "A Dozen Lords Dead In Tragic Accident!" the headline read. "A freak sandstorm at an archeological dig in Persia claimed the lives of twelve peers of the Crown earlier this week," it went on. It then listed the names of the men who had died and where they were from. Lord Craven was not on the list. She was about to set the article aside when the last line caught her eye. "Evelyn Crowley, the only child of Lord Sommers, is believed to be the only British survivor of the incident."

Evelyn felt a chill run down her spine.

Of course, she had read the newspaper articles before, many years ago. But she had distanced herself from the event so much since then, it often felt like a terrible dream. Reading the words now, holding them in her hand, made the tragedy seem so much more real.

She put the clipping aside and then rifled through the more technical paperwork deeper in the box. Papers outlining who was part of the expedition, how expenses and profits would be shared, and what would happen should any of the members suddenly die were all detailed. She could find no mention of Lord Craven anywhere.

Frustrated, she began putting the papers back into the box. It was probably for the best. What would have changed had she found out that Lord Craven had a connection to expedition anyway? Lord Craven himself was now dead as well.

As she reached for the photograph to put it back in the box, a new face stared up at her. She gasped. There, behind her father's head were two eyes and a gaping mouth. She grabbed the photograph and held it up to the light to get a better look.

She shook her head, embarrassed by her own foolishness when she saw nothing there but the rolling sand dunes behind them. It must have merely been a trick of the light. The sun was shining at a much higher angle through the window now. She had spent much more time here than she had planned. She put the last of the paper into the box, but as she started to place the photograph in it, she hesitated. She put the photograph into her pocket, closed the box, and left the room.

he doors of the library flew open and Alister breezed into the room. "Evelyn!" he demanded. "Get dressed."

Her face blushed as she looked down at her clothes. "But I am dressed, sir," she said.

Alister wrinkled his nose, and Evelyn had to concede that she hadn't put any effort into her appearance in nearly a week. She had completely lost herself in her work. She was even skipping meals so as not to be interrupted—even though Alister was always pleasant company. The dress she was wearing was her simplest frock, one she usually only wore if she knew she would be dealing with exceptionally dusty items at the museum. She wasn't even sure how the dress had made it into her case.

"Put on something nice," Alister clarified as he ushered her toward the door. "And have Susan do something with your hair. We are going out. You have been cooped up here for far too long."

"Out?" Evelyn asked. "Where? For a drive?"

"If you like," Alister said. "But then we are going to dinner."

"With other people?" she asked.

"There will be other people around," he said. "We are having dinner at the Savoy Hotel. We have reservations at eight."

"The Savoy?" Evelyn asked, her eyes wide. "Surely not. What will Mrs. Paxton think?"

Unless one was traveling, it was nearly unheard of for those of the upper-class to dine in public. It was considered an insult to the cooks and footmen in their employ.

"Don't worry yourself over Mrs. Paxton," Alister said.

"She will probably be grateful to get rid of us for an evening."

"I don't know," Evelyn said, still hesitating. What would other people think if they saw her out in public with a man she wasn't married to?

"Well, I do," Alister said. "As your patron, and your friend, I insist you join me for dinner."

"Well," Evelyn finally conceded. "If my patron insists."

The Savoy had only recently opened, but it had already become a popular gathering place for the young rich of London. Evelyn had not been there herself, but she had ridden past it many times. At eight stories tall and taking up an entire city block, it was bigger than Buckingham Palace. And with elevators, electric lights in every room, and hot water out of every tap, the hotel was a modern marvel.

Lights from inside and around the hotel lit up the city street as Evelyn and Alister stepped out of the carriage. But the beauty of the outside was nothing compared to the extravagance of the inside.

The hotel had several restaurants—a breakfast room, a tea room, and a terrace garden with a view of the river. But tonight, they would be eating in the formal dining room. The mahogany walls were ornately carved, the chairs were gilded, and the tables were covered with crisp while table clothes and set with matching bone china, crystal glasses, and engraved silverware. A full orchestra was situated on one side of the room offering ambient music and an occasional respite from conversation.

The maître d' led them to their table and then presented Alister with the wine menu.

"Have you really never dined out before?" Alister asked.

Evelyn shook her head as the maître d' placed a napkin across her lap. "Not in London," she said. "Only when I traveled abroad."

"You are certainly in for a treat," Alister said as he made the wine selection and turned to the menu. "The things that Monsieur Escoffier can do with chicken will make you forget your cook at home even exists."

"Goodness me," Evelyn said. "High praise indeed. Now I really look forward to seeing what the evening entails."

"As do I," Alister said with a mischievous smile.

The first half of the evening was taken up with enjoying the fantastic food, listening to the orchestra, and making small talk. As the night wore on, though, and the bottle of wine slowly emptied, the small talk gave way to discussions of a more scandalous nature.

"That woman there," Alister said, leaning in and whispering as he pointed across the room, "is the mistress of the Duke of Wales."

"No!" Evelyn gasped.

"And the man sitting next to her," he said. "That's Oscar Wilde."

"And me without my copy of *The Duchess of Padua*!" she lamented.

"You can bring it next time," Alister said. "He is always here."

"I do hope there is a next time," Evelyn said.

"Where do you normally go with your friends?" Alister asked.

"I...I don't really have many friends," she said, somewhat embarrassed. She must have sounded so pathetic. "Susan would be the person I am closest to."

"I am sure that Susan would be much more entertaining company than any socialite you would normally associate with," Alister said. "I bet that if you ask her where the best dance hall in London is, she could show you an exciting time."

Evelyn laughed. "Me? At a dance hall?"

Alister laughed as well. "I can just see it. You, kicking up your heels, your hair flowing freely."

Evelyn shook her head. "You are terrible."

"But you must go to the theater," Alister said. "Or have famous poets come to one of the ladies' parlor and do a reading for you?"

"Those all sound like fine things to do with friends," Evelyn said. "If I ever make any, I'll be sure to suggest them."

"You really don't associate with the other ladies?" Alister said, realizing that she wasn't joking. Evelyn shook her head. "Why not?"

"You really aren't from around here," Evelyn said. "Otherwise you surely would have heard about me. The disaster that killed my father, it led to the death of many important men. Men with children. I was the only survivor. For some reason, they seem to hold me responsible for the deaths of their fathers. Or at least, a receptacle for their anger."

Alister shook his head. "I had no idea. I'm sorry. I know how you must feel."

"Do you?" she asked, her tone coming across far more accusatorial than she meant it to.

"Yes," he said plainly. "Not to the point that I am ostracized by my peers. But I know what it is like to be blamed for the death of a loved one."

Evelyn suddenly understood his meaning. "Your father," she said. "He blamed you for your mother's death. I'm so sorry."

"Don't be," he said, reaching over and laying his hand on hers. "I have long since come to terms with it."

The warmth from Alister's hand ran through her whole body, causing her to blush.

"What about your friends?" she asked, trying to diffuse the sparks that were quickly firing between them. "I haven't noticed you going out on the town much."

"My friends are all abroad," he said. "Probably in Madrid or Verona."

"Ah," Evelyn said. "Your boarding school chums. So when you are together, what do you do?"

"We are all wealthy young men who have been disillusioned by life," he said as snobbishly as possible. "We drink absinthe under the moonlight and talk of revolution."

"It must be exquisite," Evelyn said, "to live such a Bohemian existence."

"You should try it," he said. "You traveled extensively as a girl. Don't you miss it?"

"Every day," Evelyn said without hesitation. "But, as a woman, I don't quite have the freedoms you do."

"What do you mean?" Alister asked.

Evelyn paused. Did he really not know the social constraints she had to contend with?

"I don't know what the future holds," Evelyn said. "But if I ever did decide to marry, I would need to be a woman of upstanding character."

"I am sure there are many men who do not care of such things," Alister said. "If you found a man who loved travel as much as you, he would understand that any rumors about you were simply untrue."

Evelyn wasn't sure if Alister was speaking of himself or men in general, but she noticed that his hand was still lying on hers. She looked up at his eyes, and there was no mistaking the desire there. She wondered if her eyes looked the same at that moment. She could feel a tingling in the lowest parts of her belly. Even though the table was between them, they were both leaning in toward each other. She was sure that had they been any closer together, he would have kissed her in that moment, and she would not have stopped him.

"Monsieur and madam," the maître d' said, choosing that moment to interrupt. "Is there anything else you would like this evening?"

"Only the bill," Alister said. "And our carriage."

As Alister walked her outside, her hand in the crook of his elbow, a nervousness replaced the tingling in her stomach. There was definitely an attraction building between them. And while it was not unwelcome, it could certainly complicate matters. They were living in the same house! Should Alister express interest in courting her, staying in the same home would be highly inappropriate. True, she had Susan with her, but a maid was not a chaperone. If anyone suspected that there was more to Evelyn and Alister's relationship than business, her reputation would surely be called into question. While she had considered such a risk before accepting the job, she had never imagined that Alister would show any interest in her. Now, she suddenly wondered if she would even make it back to Alister's mansion with her innocence intact.

"Monsieur," a hotel footman said to Alister as they stepped out and saw that their carriage was not waiting for them. "There is an issue with your coach. Can you come with me?"

Alister sighed in annoyance and removed her hand from his arm. "Wait here," he said. "I'm sure I won't be but a moment."

She nodded, grateful for the distance between them for a moment. She needed time to think before they ended up in the close confines of the carriage together.

She couldn't help but pace back and forth, pondering what to do, what to say, when her eyes caught sight of a shadowy figure across the street. She stared, a sense of familiarity coming over her. Was that the same person who had been watching her in the Sumerian wing at the museum?

She started to raise her hand to get the person's attention, but as soon as she moved, the person turned and ran down a nearby alley.

"Stop!" she called without thinking. Who was that person? Why was he—or she—watching her? She darted across the street. She needed to know. By the time she reached the alley, she couldn't see anyone, but she could hear footsteps running on the pavement. She followed the sound. "Hey!" she called. "Come back!"

At the end of the alley, she looked left and right, but she could see no one. Just like the night at the museum, the person had seemingly vanished.

She saw the figures of two men walking toward her, and she suddenly realized just how dark it was here. The tall buildings blocked any light from the Savoy, and there were no streetlamps. She heard a rustling noise and saw a person digging through a nearby garbage heap. She heard two dogs barking in the distance. She gulped and realized she had stupidly run into a very dangerous place. The men were getting closer, so she started to back up. But as she did, she ran into someone who grabbed her by her shoulders and turned her to face him.

"Well, well, well," the man said in a low accent. "What have we here?"

"Unhand me," she demanded, but knew her voice lacked any sense of authority.

A man behind her laughed. She turned and saw that the two men who had been some distance away were now right behind her. She was surrounded.

"Or else what?" one of the other men asked.

"My escort will be looking for me," she said. "He'll be angry with you." At least, she hoped Alister would be, once he was done being angry with her for running off like an idiot.

"Then we better leave," the first man said.

Evelyn held her breath. She doubted the men were just going to walk away.

"And take this little bird with us," another man said, grabbing her around the waist and holding her tightly.

Evelyn screamed. "Let go of me!"

The man placed a dirty hand over her mouth and pulled her so close to him he licked her cheek. She kicked her legs and tried to strike the man with her fists. But one of the other men grabbed her wrists.

"Take her here and get it over with," one of the men said.

"No, no, no!" Evelyn's muffled screams didn't carry far, but they didn't need to.

In an instant, one of the men was pulled away and shoved to the ground.

"What the—" one of the other men tried to ask, but he was silenced as Alister grabbed him and slammed his head into a wall.

The man who had Evelyn by the waist threw her to the side. She slipped on the muddy ground, landing on her knees. The man then swung a fist at Alister, but Alister easily dodged it. He grabbed the man by the jacket and slammed his face into his knee. Then he punched the man in the stomach, making him double over in pain. He then turned around and kicked the first man in the face. He grabbed the second man, who was trying to stand, and punched him once, twice, three times. Alister was in a rage.

Evelyn scrambled to her feet and grabbed Alister's elbow as he reared back to punch the man—who was begging for his life at this point—once again.

"Stop!" Evelyn said. "Let's get out of here."

"Fine," Alister said as he let go of the man and watched him slump to the ground. He then wrapped his arms around her shoulder and led her back down the alley to the Savoy.

"Madam!" the hotel footman exclaimed when he saw her. She must have looked quite a fright. "Are you all right? Shall I call the night watch?"

"I just need to take her home," Alister said.

"Yes, sir," the footman said as he opened the door to the carriage. He then quickly shut the door behind them and banged twice on the outside. The carriage took off like a shot.

"*Are* you all right?" Alister asked once they were safely on the move. "Shall I send for a doctor once we arrive home?"

"I'm fine," Evelyn said. "Just shaken. I…I'm so sorry."

"For what?" Alister asked. "Those men attacked you."

"I shouldn't have run off," she said. "I saw someone. I thought I knew—"

"It doesn't matter," Alister said. "It's not your fault.

When we get home, I'll have Mrs. Paxton send up some soothing tea while Susan tends to you."

Evelyn shook her head, ashamed he was being so kind to her when she had been so foolish. So reckless. She could have been killed! She had ruined their beautiful evening together. And for what?

She still had no idea who had been watching her.

CHAPTER TEN

*E*velyn once again closeted herself in the library, this time to hide from her shame. She wasn't literally closed away; the door was unlocked for anyone who should wish to drop by. But Evelyn found it immensely easier to lose herself in her work than have to face Alister and apologize for the hundredth time for ruining their evening together. Alister insisted she had nothing to apologize for, but she could not stop chastising herself. To quiet her brain, she focused intently on her work.

And she was sure it was paying off.

"These characters here," she said to Alister, pointing to some of her notes. "I'm certain I've seen them before."

Alister had stopped by to see how the work was progressing and had brought her a small basket of apples to ensure she wouldn't starve to death, one of which he had taken for himself. He bit into it absentmindedly as he looked at the paper.

"They all just look like lines and triangles to me," he said.

"To the untrained eye," she said with a smirk. "But if an

ancient Sumerian tried to read our writing system I'm sure it would just look like squiggles."

Alister chuckled as he tapped her nose playfully and took another bite of apple. "So, you've seen them before?" he asked. "Where?"

"Unfortunately, I can't quite remember," she said. "I'm certain I didn't see them in my own collection. It was something I saw frequently, but didn't study in detail. I think I saw them at the museum."

"So you need to go back to the museum?" he asked, leaning on her desk.

"I think so," she said. "The missing link might be there."

"The missing link?" he asked.

"Have you heard of the Rosetta Stone?" she asked.

He shrugged. "It was how people were able to understand Egyptian hieroglyphs. But I don't know the details."

"It was basically a polyglot tablet," she said. "The same information written in ancient Egyptian, a more modern but still obsolete Egyptian called demotic, and ancient Greek. Since we can still read ancient Greek, an Egyptologist named Jean-François Champollion was able to use Greek as a cipher to eventually translate the hieroglyphs."

"So you think a Rosetta Stone for ancient Sumerian is back at the museum?" Alister asked.

"Nothing as complete as the Rosetta Stone," Evelyn said. "But maybe just enough to give me the push I need."

"Well, if that is what you need to do," Alister said as he headed toward the door and polished off the apple, tossing the core into a rubbish bin. "I'll get my coat and send for the carriage."

"Wait," Evelyn said, following him. "I think...I should go alone."

"Oh?" he asked, cocking an eyebrow.

"Henry Wilkes," she said. "He is sure to be there. And, well, I do not think he likes you very much."

"I must apologize again for the way I accosted him when he was here," Alister said quickly. "I'll apologize to him again myself if I must."

"No," Evelyn said. "In truth, he and I did not leave on very good terms either. Which was unfortunate. You must understand. You know lords and ladies like us do not typically take on an occupation. And women of any class are discouraged from working outside the home. Henry Wilks was the only person who gave me the opportunity to use my skills in translation and my knowledge of the world in a real and meaningful way. I owe him for that."

"You don't *owe* people who treat you like a thinking human being," Alister said. "It should be a basic requirement of anyone who wishes to interact with other people."

Evelyn chuckled to hide tears that threatened to burst forth. "You can't imagine what it means to me to hear someone say that. You must know how difficult it is for us women to be taken seriously."

Alister sighed. "I do. I like to pretend that just because I treat women with respect that everyone else in the world does too. But I know that is not the truth."

"Even if I never go back to work at the museum, having a friend there could be advantageous for me," she went on. "Such as when I need to examine the museum's collections to find a missing link."

Alister took her hand in his and then lifted it to his mouth. Her stomach turned to jelly in that moment.

"Very well," he said with a dejected sigh. "If you think it would be better for you to go alone, I'll not complicate matters for you."

"You are not the person adding complications to my life," Evelyn said.

"Am I not?" he asked, rubbing the back of her hand against his cheek. "I must not be trying hard enough."

Evelyn's mouth went dry and she struggled to find the right words. But she didn't need them. Alister pulled her close to him and gently placed his lips on hers.

He tasted sweet, like the apple he had just been eating. She loved apples. He placed both of his hands on her jaw and kissed her slightly harder. She knew she should protest, but she didn't want to. She wanted him. She closed her eyes and let go. She felt tremors in her stomach and pinpricks run down her back. She slightly opened her mouth to take more of him in.

He pulled back and looked down at her, a hunger in his eyes. She almost thought she heard him growl.

"Should I apologize?" he whispered.

"Never," she said.

"Did that complicate matters enough for you?" he asked in his normal voice, stepping away and unhanding her. She immediately felt the loss of him and almost lost her balance. She cleared her throat and ran her hands down the front of her gown.

"It certainly put matters in a new light," she said. "You know such actions are inappropriate considering our current working and living arrangements."

"Inappropriate enough to send you running back home?" he asked.

"Certainly not," she said. "My desire to find out the contents of that book outweigh any concerns over your rakish behavior."

"I'm a rake, now am I?" he asked, giving her a mischievous smile that made her weak in the knees. She placed a hand on a nearby shelf to give her strength.

"Are you?" she asked. "Am I merely a game to you? Someone to conquest? Or is there something...more between us?"

"I think you already know there is something far more happening between us," he said.

"Then what are we to do about it?" she asked. "A formal courtship? Should I return home? I am afraid I don't know the rules."

"Dash the rules," he said. "I'm not proposing marriage." Her heart dropped, and she was sure it showed on her face. "I'm not proposing marriage *yet*," he clarified. "I'm not opposed to the idea, but I am certainly in no rush. Are you?"

"Lucky for you, I am not," she said. "I told you, this translation, it could take years. I plan to see it through."

"Then I see no reason to change how things are," he said. "Just two people who enjoy each other's company and want to get to know one another. And should we happen to enjoy the occasional physical exchange of affection..." He twisted a lock of her hair around one of his fingers. "Well, who outside these walls would be any the wiser?"

She felt her face go hot and she gulped, looking down. "You know that there are certain...boundaries that cannot be crossed," she said, begging the stars that he not ask her to explain. She barely knew more than the scientific aspects of lovemaking and was not of a mind to discuss them so openly. While she was beyond merely attracted to Alister and found the idea of falling into bed with him more than a little appealing, she knew that far too many men in this world still preferred virgin brides. It would be in her best interest to remain as such in case her relationship with Alister didn't head in that direction.

Who was she fooling? She had to remain chaste. Alister wouldn't seriously want to marry her. He was probably only attracted to her because of their near proximity. As soon as she finished translating the book, he would be off once again to some exotic land and forget all about her.

But why shouldn't she enjoy his attention while it lasted?

"I promise I will never do anything you are not comfortable with," Alister said. "Where is the pleasure if both parties are not in enjoyment?"

"Then I look forward to getting to know you even better," Evelyn said. "As soon as I return from my trip to the museum *alone*."

"Damn," Alister said, feinting anger. "I was hoping you had forgotten all about that."

"Not a chance," Evelyn said with a laugh.

*A*s she rode in Alister's carriage to the museum, Evelyn knew her mind was not where it should be. She needed to be thinking about her translation and what to be on the look at for at the museum. She needed to think about how she was going to ask Henry for his help without revealing too much about her work.

But all she could think about was Alister. His touch. His taste. His smile. How much she enjoyed his company. How she could almost imagine a life with him. He hated London and loved to travel. He respected her work and was educated enough to have engaging conversations about it.

They could travel the world together and never stop learning.

Oh, what a pretty dream it was. But she was getting much too far ahead of herself. As Alister had said, they were simply two people getting to know each other. Whether there was a future between them was too far off in the distance to tell. She needed to focus on the book for now.

She wondered if this was what falling in love was like. It was wild and dangerous and distracting. And she realized why people did it over and over again. It was thrilling. Exhilarating. It was nearly as exciting as discovering a new language. And that was what she needed to focus on. As the coach pulled up in front of the museum, she checked for the thirtieth time that she had all of her notes in her bag and then stepped out.

It felt strange coming to the museum as a guest and not for work, and stranger still coming after such a long absence. How long had it been? She had so often lost track of the days lately. She knew it had been at least weeks since she last left the museum, if not longer. It had been early summer when she first received Alister's summons. It was now nearly autumn. Had months already passed?

Would Henry be happy to see her? Would he still be angry? Well, no time to wonder. She needed to find that missing link, and she would have to do whatever Henry wanted in order to get to it.

She had barely stepped foot in the front door, taking a deep breath of the familiar smells of dust and old books, when she saw Henry climbing down the stairs and heading straight toward her. She hadn't told him she was coming. He must have seen her arrive from an upstairs window.

"Evelyn!" he said as he approached, his hands

outstretched and a smile on his face. She smiled back and took his hands in hers. She allowed him to kiss her cheek, though it was an unwelcome exchange with the taste of Alister still on her tongue.

"Henry," she said. "How are you?"

"A world happier now that you are here," he said, wrapping her hand in the crook of his arm and leading her into the museum. "It has been frightfully dull without you working by my side."

She felt a sudden pang of guilt and looked down to hide her wavering smile. She'd barely spared a thought for him since their last parting, even though they had worked together for years before that. While her new working arrangement was somewhat lonelier, it was preferable knowing that in the end, she would receive proper credit for her work.

"Well, I am here now," she finally said. "For the afternoon, anyway."

"Oh, so you haven't completed whatever task old Lord Craven set for you?" Henry asked, fishing for information about the job.

"Far from it," Evelyn said, pulling out her notebook but keeping it closed for now. "I have made some gains, but I believe there might be an item here in the museum that can help me."

"What item?" Henry asked.

"That's the problem," she said. "I'm not quite sure." She opened her notebook and turned to the page with the characters in question. "I'm sure I've come across this writing pattern before. The images would be slightly different, of course. But there should be enough similarities between this and high Sumerian to devise a meaning, don't you think?"

Henry looked at the paper and rubbed his chin. Evelyn was sure he could not make heads or tails of it, but he had to put on a show of understanding it.

"So, you are looking for an item here in the museum with this same writing pattern but with different, even more archaic characters?" he finally asked.

Evelyn sighed as she took the paper back. "That's the long and short of it I'm afraid."

Henry chuckled. "Darling, you know we have countless items here. Each one you've spent hours looking at. It could be anywhere."

Ignoring his use of the word darling, Evelyn nodded. "I know, but nothing about this task has been simple. If it takes me days to find it and weeks to decipher the meaning, I'll have to do it."

Henry's face brightened at that, no doubt thrilled at the idea of having her back at the museum for weeks. He probably thought he could use that time to woo her back to working with him—*volunteering*, that is—instead of for Lord Craven. Well, as far as Evelyn was concerned, there was nothing he could do or say to convince her to stay, but she would have to play nice and let him think he had a ghost of a chance if she wanted access to the museum's collection.

"Let's get to work then," Henry said, motioning toward the stairs that led to the Sumerian wing. "Would you like some tea? I remember just how you like it."

"That sounds lovely," Evelyn said as she stood in front of the first exhibit, her pencil at the ready. Henry then left her in blessed peace and quiet for a moment to fetch the tea.

Evelyn looked around the large exhibition hall. Of course, this was only what the museum had on display. There were hundreds, if not thousands more items in storage in the basement and attic. Not to mention shelves upon shelves of scrolls and books. It was a ridiculously monumental task to think she could happen to find this small bit of particular phrasing somewhere in the museum —and that it would suddenly help her make sense of practically a whole new language. Goodness, what had she set herself up for?

Yet, just as she was feeling dismayed, she remembered what brought her here in the first place. The phrasing she was looking for wasn't random—it was familiar. She had seen it before, and many times. It was like a famous quote that sits just on the tip of your tongue. You know it is there, you just can't recall it in the moment. But if you think about it long enough, it will come to you eventually. She knew that if she returned to this familiar place, surrounded herself with items she knew well, she would remember where she had seen the pattern before. She simply had to be patient.

She took a deep breath and steeled herself for the task ahead. She pulled out her notes and looked at the first exhibit, a cuneiform tablet. But as she looked at it, her eyes shifted their focus on a reflection in the glass. She looked up and saw an old vase. She nearly ignored it, but something stopped her. She thought back to the last time she had been in this room. The night of the gala when she had seen Jane Poole. She had rushed up here to be alone. But she wasn't alone. She had been looking at that vase when she realized she was being watched.

She walked over to the vase and skimmed over it—as she had done hundreds of times before. She then remembered why she only ever skimmed it. She couldn't read it. It was certainly a Sumerian artifact, but the writing was so archaic, no one knew what was written on it.

But Evelyn knew.

There, on a prominent curve of the vase's neck, was the same pattern she had written in her notes. A pattern she had devised from the book. This was what she was looking for!

She heard the tinkling of a tea tray as Henry entered the room. "Henry!" she exclaimed, causing him to nearly drop the tea things. "Come here. Bring your keys!"

Henry put the tray down and rushed to her side. "What is it?" he asked.

"This," she said pointing to the vase. "This is it."

"You found it already?" he asked, rummaging in his pocket for the keys.

"Yes, yes," she said, shaking her hands and shifting from one foot to the other. "Oh please. Please!"

Henry opened the display case and Evelyn reached for the vase. She had to stop herself, willing her hands to stop shaking lest she drop it. She picked it up and it was heavier than she imagined. She walked over to the table with the tea things and placed it there. She turned the vase around, and she could have cried when she saw it.

The exact same text was written on the other side of the vase in high Sumerian. She could read it.

"Oh my God," she exclaimed. "I found it! The Rosetta Stone!"

"What?" Henry asked. "What do you mean? You can read it?"

"This half," Evelyn explained, "is written in high Sumerian, which, yes, I can read. The other half is written in the even older archaic Sumerian, the same as the book I'm translating for Al...for Lord Craven. I can't read the archaic Sumerian, not yet. But this is the key!"

"That is fantastic!" Henry said. "You must stay here and

work on this. Such a discovery will bring so much prestige to the museum. We must have more archaic items for you to compare it with."

Evelyn pulled out more notepaper and began writing furiously. "Oh no," she said. "I must get back to the book. This changes everything."

"But, your skills will surely go to waste on such a trifling project," Henry said as he picked up one of her note pages. "Working for one person is nothing like working for such a esteemed museum as this one."

"Would I be allowed to work here?" Evelyn asked as she continued sketching. "Or just volunteer."

"Evelyn," Henry chided. "You know how things work."

"I do," she said. "Which is why I must get back to the book."

"Evelyn," Henry said, pulling on her shoulders, forcing her to face him and scattering her papers on the floor. "Come to your senses. You had your fun. But you have made a brilliant discovery. You belong here."

"And as soon as I finish compiling a dictionary and complete my first translation, I would be happy to go to the museum directors myself and present my findings," Evelyn said.

Henry's nostrils flared. He was not pleased that she would be going over his head in order to get credit for her discovery. But Evelyn would not back down. Not now. What she had done, he could never have done in a million years. He would not be able to take this accomplishment away from her. He stared down at her, and she met his gaze with equal force. Eventually, he released her arms from his grip.

"Fine," he said. "But the vase is the property of the museum. You cannot take it with you."

"I don't need it," she said as she bent down to pick up her papers. "I have everything I need."

Henry stooped down and helped her, handing her the small stack.

"I do hope you won't forget me when you are standing in your ivory tower looking down on the rest of us," he said sullenly.

Evelyn put her papers into her bag and clasped it closed.

"I won't be in an ivory tower," she said. "I'll be in Carnarvon Castle."

With that, she held her head high, turned on her heels, and walked out of the room. She hoped she would never have to see Henry Wilkes again.

CHAPTER ELEVEN

*B*ack at the house, Evelyn worked late into the night. To Mrs. Paxton's horror, Evelyn had requested coffee after dinner instead of tea to help her stay up later so she could work uninterrupted. The discovery of the Vase of Babylon—as Evelyn decided to call it; she knew the vase would need a name as catchy as Rosetta Stone in order for the magnitude of its importance to be appreciated—had changed everything, and she didn't want to waste a moment when she could be working on the translation.

She was still far from understanding the text. But the vase allowed her to start working up a sort of dictionary. She needed to understand the words individually. Then she could piece the words together to form sentences. It was an arduous process, but she had gotten farther than any other researcher of archaic Sumerian before her. She was on the right path; she just needed to stay the course.

She was on her third cup of coffee, and she grimaced as she drank the bitter brew.

"Blech," she said as she put the cup down. "Wretched.

How do Americans drink this stuff? Okay, work, work, work. Words, words, words."

She chanted to herself, trying to keep up the motivation to keep going. The clock on the wall struck four o'clock, and she knew it was four in the morning, not the afternoon. She should go to bed, but she wouldn't be able to sleep. Her mind would spin and she would toss and turn and awaken no more rested than she was now, so she might as well keep working.

As she continued talking to herself, she heard a low humming sound, as though hundreds of bees were beating their wings nearby. Evelyn rubbed her eyes, wondering if she was dreaming the strange noise, but the humming continued. She stood and walked over to a window. The noise got slightly louder. It was incredibly dark outside. She could only see her reflection in the window as she tried to look outside. She unfastened the latch and pushed the window open. A stiff cool breeze rushed in, fluttering her hair and the folds of her dress and sending a chill through her. She shuddered. But the humming grew louder.

"What *is* that?" she asked no one. She strained her ears and realized that it wasn't humming she was hearing, but chanting. She couldn't make out the words, but the sound was unmistakable. It was similar to the chanting of monks she heard when she visited the Vatican on her long trek to the Near East.

But who would be chanting out here? There was no monastery that she knew of. And at four in the morning? It was too early even for Matins.

Suddenly, she felt uneasy. As though she shouldn't be prying into whatever secret rite this was. She leaned through the pane to grab the window, which had flown as wide open as possible. She stretched and strained to grab hold, but her fingers could barely reach the handle. She leaned forward a little more. A little too far! Losing her balance, she started to tumble forward.

She screamed as a hand fell on her shoulder.

"M'lady!" Susan yelled as she pulled Evelyn back into the room. "What in heaven's name! You nearly fell through."

"Oh, Susan," Evelyn gasped as she pulled her maid in for a hug. "It's only you."

"Who else would it be at this ungodly hour?" Susan asked, pulling her shawl around her.

"Quite," Evelyn said. "I can't quite close the window, and I don't want to leave it open."

Susan stepped forward and leaned out, grabbing the window with ease and pulling it closed, locking it tightly.

"I never realized you had such long arms," Evelyn said jokingly.

"They run in the family," Susan said. "Why was it open anyway? It gets terribly gusty at night around here."

"I thought I heard something," Evelyn said, looking back to the window, but only able to see her reflection once again. "A...a humming sound."

"Humming?" Susan asked. "Well, I don't know about that. But you shouldn't be up so late anyway. Come on."

"I—" Evelyn started to protest, but then she realized that she indeed was a bit tired. So she allowed Susan to cart her off upstairs and pack her away in bed for the night.

The next day, Evelyn found it impossible to concentrate. Her mind was abuzz with activity, but she couldn't focus on the work itself. She felt adrift, her mind floating from one thing to another, unable to stay in one place for very long.

She stared out the window, toward where the mysterious sound was coming from as she sipped her morning tea. Everything seemed completely normal now. No strange sounds, no ominous lights. She must have been seeing things. Or sleepwalking. It had been four a.m. Her exhausted mind had been surely playing tricks on her. Even now, it still refused to settle and let her work.

"M'lady," Susan said, entering the room. "Are you sure you won't rest? You were up so late and then awoke at your usual time. Mr. Shaw will not begrudge you taking a day off. He'd be glad of it."

"I'm sure he would," Evelyn said, finishing her tea and placing the cup and saucer on the edge of her desk. "Where is Mr. Shaw? He wasn't at breakfast."

"I don't rightly know," Susan said. "I just heard he went to town. I didn't ask why."

Of course she didn't, as it wasn't her business. Neither was is Evelyn's, though she couldn't help but be curious.

"Will you walk with me, Susan?" Evelyn asked.

"A walk, ma'am?" Susan asked, surprised. "Outside?"

"That is where one usually takes walks," Evelyn said.

Susan blushed. "Of course, ma'am," she said. "I was only surprised. I don't think you've left the house except to get in a coach to go to town."

"Right," Evelyn said, more determined. "It is time that changed. I've been here...how many months? And I haven't even explored the gardens."

"Well, *you* haven't, ma'am," Susan said. Evelyn cocked an eyebrow at her. "Just because you've taken up the life of a hermit doesn't mean I have."

"Quite," Evelyn said. "Well, you shall give me the grand tour then."

"Of course, ma'am," Susan said. "Let me go back upstairs and grab you a shawl. It's right chilly this morning."

Evelyn and Susan went out the back of the house, where the garden sprawled for quite a distance. However, Evelyn was sad to discover that the garden—like much of the rest of the house—had not been well tended to. The grass was short, but in the planting areas where roses and other flowers once bloomed where now grey and overgrown with thorns and weeds.

"Doesn't Mr. Shaw employ a gardener?" Evelyn asked as she reached out and took the dead, dry remains of a flower in her fingers and crushed it, letting the chaff drift away in the breeze.

"I'd call him more of a groundskeeper," Susan said. "He cuts the grass and trims the hedges, but he doesn't seem interested in the care and cultivation of the garden beds."

"Tragic," Evelyn said. At one time, one of the Lady Cravens must have taken a great interest in the garden. Evelyn could see the skeleton of what was one a lush and layered garden with countess varieties of flowers and vining plants growing in harmony with one another.

"Perhaps you could convince him to hire a proper gardener," Susan said as they left the garden and headed out across the wide lawn.

"Me?" Evelyn asked incredulously. "Why me?"

"It's fairly clear he is smitten with you, m'lady," Susan said. "I'd almost say you have him wrapped around your finger."

Evelyn sputtered a laugh. "What? Never!"

"It's true!" Susan said. "Do...do you really not see it?"

"See what?" Evelyn asked.

"The way he looks at you," Susan said. "The way he dotes on you. The way he touches your hand or your shoulder when he is near you. He's smitten!"

Evelyn felt her heart flutter. Of course she hoped it was true. And to hear it from someone else, well, at least she wasn't imagining things.

"He has been very kind," Evelyn admitted. "Flirtatious, even, I'll admit. But..."

"But what?" Susan asked.

"Do you not think that maybe he is just being..." She hated to say it, but Susan encouraged her with her eyes. "That maybe he is just a rake. That he only wants to seduce me. Have some fun while we are under the same roof."

Susan nodded. "We must always be careful of dangerous men," she said. "But you can't see his face when you back is turned. How he can't tear his eyes away until you are well out of view. How while you are working, he paces the halls just looking for an excuse to bother you. How even when you are not hungry, he makes sure that your place is set at dinner, just in case you make time for him."

Evelyn's hand flew to her mouth. "Oh dear! Have I been a terrible guest? Have I been cruel to him? I didn't know!"

Susan laughed. "Make him wait! You are working. You're not here for his pleasure. And the more he waits, the more he will appreciate you when you do grace him with your presence."

"Oh, Susan," Evelyn sighed, taking her friend's hand in her arm. "I could never imagine a man like that looking twice at me, much less pacing the halls for want of me."

"I'm so happy for you, ma'am," Susan said, squeezing Evelyn's arm. "He's a dream! Rich and handsome. And smart enough not to be intimidated by how smart you are."

"Sounds like you've been spending a lot of time thinking about Mr. Shaw yourself," Evelyn teased.

Susan laughed. "Well, I don't have much else to occupy my time with here. But don't worry about me, ma'am. I have a beau of my own."

"You do?" Evelyn asked, surprised. "Why haven't you mentioned him before? What's his name?"

"His name is Geoffrey," Susan said. "He's a footman for Mr. Drew, a wealthy merchant in Manchester."

"You are from Manchester, right?" Evelyn asked. "Did you meet him on a trip home?"

"Oh, we've known each other for an age," Susan said. "Our mums are neighbors."

"Oh, that's lovely," Evelyn said. "Your mother must be so pleased."

"She is," Susan said, then her smile faltered a little, and Evelyn thought she knew why.

"Does this mean you are going to leave me?" Evelyn asked.

"No, ma'am," Susan said. "Not soon. Being in service makes it hard to have a family of one's own."

Evelyn nodded. It was an unfortunate truth of life. The upper class relied on their servants from dawn till dusk, if not twenty-four hours a day. It was difficult for servants to find time for courtship, marriage, and their own lives while waiting hand and foot on someone else. Not to mention trying to have children.

"Please, don't put your own life on hold for me," Evelyn said. "While I would be sad to lose you, you deserve to have your own life."

"That's very kind, ma'am," Susan said. "But that's not why we've had to delay the marriage. Neither of us can afford to leave service. I'd like him to get a placement here in London, but Mr. Drew has been good to Geoffrey."

"He's not by chance interested in becoming a gardener, is he?" Evelyn asked. "Perhaps I could use my powers of persuasion over Mr. Shaw to bring him on here."

They laughed together.

"He's not a gardener," Susan finally said. "But...if you could help Geoffrey make introductions here in the city, we'd be right grateful."

"I'll see what I can do," Evelyn said. Unfortunately, she didn't think she was on good enough terms with anyone in the city to recommend a servant to them, but she would keep her eye out for opportunities.

"What is that?" Susan asked.

Evelyn looked in the direction Susan was pointing and saw an old Near Eastern-looking structure. Evelyn knew that gardens of large estates usually had faux ruins and other classical structures, so at first, she thought nothing of it. But as they walked closer, Evelyn noticed a low wall covered in moss and vines. They looked over the wall and saw several gravestones.

"This must be the Shaw family graveyard," Evelyn said.

"A graveyard? "Susan said, crossing herself. "Oh, I don't really like the sound of that."

Evelyn nodded, but was intrigued by the large structure. She stepped closer to it, but Susan grabbed her arm.

"What are you doing?" Susan asked.

"I just want to get a closer look," Evelyn said, removing Susan's hand. They walked along the wall until they found an opening and a cobblestone path. Evelyn followed the path, but Susan stayed well outside the border wall.

"I'll just wait here," Susan said, shifting from one foot to the next uncomfortably.

Evelyn nodded. As she got closer to the structure, she realized it was a crypt. It had the name Shaw written above the door in large bold letters. But the crypt looked new. She then noticed that there were Sumerian characters carved on either side of the door. They were not high Sumerian, but the archaic Sumerian she was studying now. She couldn't make out the meaning.

She thought that this must be the eternal resting place of Alister's father, Bannister Shaw. His love for the old Sumerian book would explain the odd appearance of the crypt. She turned and looked back toward the house. She could barely see it from here, but from what she could see, she realized that the graveyard was on the side of the house where the library was.

She felt a cold chill creep over her shoulder and down her back, right into her bones. The mysterious chanting sounds had come from this direction!

A scream rent the air, and Evelyn gasped. Susan!

She ran back down the path out of the graveyard.

"Susan?" She yelled.

"Oh, m'lady!" Susan cried, turning toward her. "Can I keep it?" There in Susan's arms was a small tabby kitten.

Evelyn sighed with relief. "That was a scream to wake the dead!" she said, panting as though she had just run a mile.

"I'm so sorry," Susan said. "I just got so excited when I saw her. Isn't she darling? And out here all alone!"

Evelyn looked around and made a clicking noise with her tongue. It was odd. She didn't see any other cats or a barn where a cat might live. Where was the kitten's mother?

"Can't we bring it back with us?" Susan asked. "We can't leave her out here in the cold."

Evelyn hesitated, looking around once more in vain for the mother cat.

"Well," she finally said. "We can't just leave it here now that you've fallen in love with it."

"I'm so sorry, m'lady," Susan said. "It happened so fast."

Evelyn laughed and turned Susan back toward the house. "Yes," she said. "I suppose love does often sneak upon us like that."

CHAPTER TWELVE

"I've done it!" Evelyn cried, standing up triumphantly as she stared down at her work. She ran to the door and threw it open. "Alister!" She called. "Come quickly!"

To her surprise, Alister was just down the hall, as though waiting for her call. Maybe there was something to what Susan said about him being anxious to see her. But she couldn't think of that right now.

"What is it?" Alister asked as he briskly walked to the library.

She took him by the hand and dragged him to the desk. "I've done it!" She said again. "I've cracked the language. I've figured it out."

Alister laughed and hugged her. "That's brilliant, darling! What does it say?"

"Oh," she said, as though surprised he would ask. "Well, I can't quite read it yet."

"But you said..." he started to say but let the words die away. He knew he didn't really understand her process.

"You said you speak French, right?" Evelyn asked,

walking over to a shelf and grabbing a random French book.

"Yes," he said.

Evelyn opened the book and grabbed a piece of paper. She copied the first couple of sentences of the book to the paper, but she only copied the letters, evenly spaced, with no capitalization or punctuation. She handed it to him.

"There, can you read that?" She asked.

Alister smiled as though this was a silly game, but as he looked at the paper, the smile fled from his lips.

"Umm...with great difficulty," he admitted.

"That is the stage I am at now with this book," Evelyn said. "I have the 'letters,' so to speak. But I still have to discern the meaning."

"It looks like you still have quite a job ahead of you," Alister said. "But you've come so far! This is still wonderful. Will you let me take you out to celebrate? A play and then dinner at the Savoy. Please say yes."

"Oh, I couldn't possibly," Evelyn said. "This is just so incredible. I'm so close."

"I understand that this is exciting," Alister said with a bit more severity. "But I worry about you. When was the last time you left the house? You barely eat and hardly sleep. This schedule can't be good for you." He reached up and cupped her cheek in his hand.

Evelyn closed her eyes and nestled into his touch. It was so warm and comforting. If only she could feel that touch all over her...

She forced her eyes to open. She couldn't lose sight of her goal. Not now.

"I'm sorry," she said. "I don't want to lose the momentum. Just let me get started on the first page..." Alister raised his eyebrow at her. "The first paragraph?" Somehow, he raised his eyebrow even higher. "The title? Please, just the title, and then we will have dinner together."

Alister let out a long sigh. "Fine," he said. "Just the title. Then dinner. I'm going to hold you to that. If you are not at the table at precisely seven o'clock, I shall carry you to the table myself."

"I certainly hope you do," Evelyn said playfully.

Alister stepped close and took her face in his hands. "I knew you could do it." He then leaned in and kissed her lightly on the nose, as though he knew that a kiss on the lips could completely undo her and leave her unable to work. He then left the room, closing the doors behind him.

Evelyn sighed, then she nearly danced back over to her desk. Everything was perfect right now, in this moment. And it would only get better. Once she had translated the book, she could send her findings on her translation of archaic Sumerian to various history and language experts around the world for review. Once they verified her claims, various publications would want to share her discovery with the world! Or so she hoped. The importance of the discoveries of lost languages and cultures was often lost on the average person. She could only dream that people would care about the Vase of Babylon as much as they did about the Rosetta Stone.

Well, there would be time to worry about that later. For now, she needed to get the translation done.

She sat back down and got to work on the very first page. Even for her, with her skill and excitement, it was a grueling tedious process. By the time seven o'clock rolled around, she didn't even have the complete title translated. She only knew it was something about a powerful king.

As soon as dinner was over, she went back to the library,

determined to get the title translated before she went to bed.

And she finally did, but she was shocked at what she saw the book was about.

The Evil King and the Curse the People Did Lay Upon Him.

CHAPTER THIRTEEN

*T*here was once a great and powerful king who ruled over all of Mesopotamia. None before him had united all the people of the Persia and the Orient. Under him, there was much peace and prosperity.

But his sons were lazy. Selfish. Spoiled. Three sons the king had, and all were born after the king had achieved his greatness. The sons did not know war, or hunger, or struggle. The sons only fought each other, because each one thought he should be the one to inherit their father's kingdom.

"As the eldest, I should inherit," said the king's firstborn.

"But I am the strongest," said the second born. "No man in the land can best me."

"But I am the smartest," said the third born. "I have learned from the greatest thinkers of our time."

"What does being born earn you?" The king asked his first-born. "What did you accomplish by coming out of your mother's womb?"

This caused the firstborn to seethe.

"And so what if you are strong?" The king asked his second born. "What do you know of military strategy? Have you ever *fought with anyone besides your brothers for the last sweetmeat at supper?"*

This caused the second born great embarrassment.

"And so what if great teachers have imparted their wisdom to you?" He asked his third born. "What wise thoughts have originated with you?"

This caused the third born great sadness.

"Perhaps," said the queen, in her desire to see peace in her home, "you could give each of our sons an inheritance. Surely the kingdom is large enough for each son to rule his own land."

"No!" the king yelled without even considering the suggestion. "I will not tear asunder what I have built with my own hand. I would rather live forever than divide my kingdom or leave it to any of these worthless pups I have sired."

So that is what the king determined to do. He must live forever if he wished to see his kingdom remain whole and under the hand of a capable ruler.

To live forever became his obsession.

He opened the gates to the city and invited every mystic, shaman, and witch in the region—regardless of the god or creed the person followed—to come to him and perform their spells and rituals to make him live forever. If any mystic succeeded in making him immortal, he would reward the person with riches, honor, and power beyond their wildest dreams.

But if they failed, they would be executed in the most horrid way imaginable.

The risk was great, but still many who claimed to have magical abilities flocked to the capital city for a chance to make the king immortal.

Anything the mystics told the king to do, he did.

The first mystic told him he needed to slaughter one thousand cows on the nearby sacred mountain under a full moon and bathe in the animals' blood.

Even though it would lead to severe food shortage, the king did this.

But he continued to age.

He had the mystic impaled on a stake and left to rot in the city square.

Another mystic told him to drink a powerful potion. He did this. He not only continued to age, but was severely ill for many days. There was even a fear that the king would die.

But then king did not die. Instead, he had the mystic boiled alive in oil in the city square.

Another mystic told him to shed his own blood under a harvest moon while standing in the sacred river.

The king stood in the river and sliced his own wrist, letting the blood pool down his arm and then dissolving in the healing waters below him.

But still, he grew older.

He had the mystic flayed alive in the city square.

For many years after this, no mystics came to the city. Some believed his proclamation had actually been a trick to purge the country of witchcraft.

Finally, in an act of desperation, the king announced that whoever was able to make him immortal, he would make her a queen by allowing her to marry his oldest son.

From a desert and an ocean away, a beautiful enchantress dared to make the perilous journey and risk the wrath of the king —She of the Moon and Stars.

In the throne room, before the king, the queen, their three sons, and all the important people of the land, the enchantress told the king what must be done.

"I know how to make you immortal," the enchantress said. "But it will come at great personal sacrifice."

"Whatever you say, I will do," the king said, his now grey beard so long it nearly dragged the floor.

"You must kill your youngest son," the enchantress said, "and drink his blood, then you will live forever."

"Vile creature!" the queen said, jumping to her feet. "You speak the word of the devil!"

"Father," the third son gasped. "This woman is insane."

But the king was not so sure she was. He stroked his long beard.

"What you say is truly shocking, woman," he said. "How can I believe your words?"

"All gods require blood to prove sincerity," she said. "Of course, they would require the greatest sacrifice to give you the ultimate gift."

"Husband," the queen said, gripping her husband's arm, "you cannot do this!"

"Father," the youngest son said. "Will you not throw this beggar witch out for saying such wicked things?"

The king's older sons, though, remained silent.

"Who is the truly wicked one?" the king asked. "Will my other sons not speak up for their brother? Had she asked for the eldest, would you have also stayed silent, my third born?"

"This is preposterous!" the queen said. "The sacrifice of any of our children is too much to ask. Send her away."

"I agree, my pet," the king said, patting his queen consolingly on the hand. "The sacrifice of our children is far too much."

At that, the king had to enchantress led away, but he did not banish her or execute her. Instead, he had her secreted away to a temple at the edge of the city.

"Do you swear to me," the king asked, "that if I do this, I will become immortal? Do you know the hell you will suffer if you fail me?"

The enchantress opened her hands and stars flew out of them, embedding themselves in the black heaven above.

"I swear it," she said.

At that, the king ordered his guards to find a beautiful virgin maid from a nearby village. He caged her in a locked room below the temple. The room was beautiful, with the finest rugs and decorations one could dream of. He provided her with the most delectable foods she could ever imagine.

And there, he raped her. Every night for many weeks, he would visit the girl and force himself upon her until finally, she was with child.

For nine months, the king waited for the birth of his child—one he hoped would be his youngest son. A son he never met or cared for. One bred for the express purpose of being sacrificed in the name of his father.

The girl, of course, had no idea what the king was planning. She only thought the king was a cruel monster. But she believed that when her child was born, she and the babe would be freed and ensconced in the palace as a mistress and bastard child of a king should be.

The child was born under a harvest moon. One as high, bright, and yellow as a dog's eyes in the sky.

Through great pain, the young girl brought forth a son into the world. She held him close, smelled his hair, and let him suckle at her breast.

"Look, great king, what I have brought forth for you," the girl said through her tears. "A son!"

The king took the baby into his arms and then walked out of the room.

"Wait!" the girl cried. "Where are you taking him? Stop!"

She grabbed the king's arm, tugging, begging for her child. The king struck her across the face, leaving her unconscious in the doorway of her cell.

In the main temple hall, the king presented the squealing infant to the enchantress. She brought forth a dagger, said magical words over it, and then plunged the knife into the heart *of the baby. She collected the blood in a holy goblet of gold and presented it to the king. The king guzzled the warm liquid like a hungry child. He fell to the floor and writhed, screaming out in great pain.*

Then he felt nothing.

"What have you done, witch?" he asked.

"Exactly as you have asked of me," she said.

He looked at his hands, still withered, and his beard, still white. "But I am still old," he said.

"You asked for immortality," the enchantress said, "not your youth restored. Now give me that which was promised."

"Then what was the point?" The king roared. "Unlimited years without youthful vigor? You've tricked me!"

"I did nothing of the sort!" the enchantress said. "Now pay your debt."

"Kill her!" the king ordered his guards.

But with a flick of her wrist, the enchantress snuffed out the lives of the king's men. Then she vanished into thin air.

"A curse upon you, old king..." her voice whispered on the air.

The king wandered back to his castle in despair.

But he had forgotten about the girl from the village.

In his haste to wrest the baby from her, he had not secured the door to her cell. She had looked on in helpless horror as the king killed her child.

Still in her birthing clothes and without her shoes, wailing her unimaginable pain, she wandered back to her village.

The people were shocked when she returned alive. After being missing for so long, they thought her surely dead. But their shock turned to horror as she told them of her imprisonment, her abuse, and the murder of her baby, all at the hands of their king.

"The king is a monster!" the people cried. Rumors of him slipping from sanity had circulated for many years, but this abhorrent crime against one of their own could not stand!

Together, they gathered weapons and marched on the king's castle.

The people broke through the king's guards and stormed the throne room. There, the father of the mistreated girl impaled the king with a lance through the heart. The king stumbled and fell, but he did not die. He pulled the lance from his chest.

The enchantment had worked. And more than that, it made the king strong.

The king then turned his full wrath on the people, slaughtering them one by one. He laughed as he stood over their desecrated corpses.

"Who can stop me now?" he yelled. "I shall rule the world!"

The king's sons were disgusted over what their father had done to their baby brother.

"Who can trust him?" the oldest son asked.

"He is surely mad," the second one said.

"We must stop him," the third one said.

Together, the three sons turned on their father.

But they could not defeat him. The king turned on his sons.

"What need have I for an heir now?" he asked as they begged for their lives. He laughed and set their heads upon pikes in the city square.

The queen was overwrought with pain for the loss of her sons. In the darkness of night, she donned a cloak and went in search of the enchantress. She found her returned to the cursed temple.

"Enchantress!" the queen begged as she fell to her knees. "I know your power is true. But my husband the king has betrayed all of us. Give me the means to end his life."

"I cannot," the enchantress said. "What is done cannot be undone."

"There must be a way," the queen said.

The enchantress pulled out a dagger, ornately decorated and carved with ancient runes, and said a curse over it.

"Plunge this dagger into his heart," the enchantress said. "It will kill his body, but not his soul. He will be forced to wander the earth for eternity in never-ending torment."

Th queen eagerly took the dagger. "A quick death would be too good for him," she said. "He should suffer until the end of time for the deaths of our sons."

The queen put the dagger into her cloak and returned to the castle.

That night, the king came to the queen's side.

"You are all I have left," the king cooed, running a finger along her chin. "The only one who has not betrayed me."

"But you have betrayed me," the queen said. With that, she pulled out the dagger and stabbed the king in the heart.

The king stumbled and fell. And this time he did not get up. He truly was dead. But the queen looked around her, at the loss of her husband, her king, her children, and her kingdom. She could not live with the guilt of what her husband had done and the loss of her children.

She raised the dagger high, cursed her husband one last time, and plugged the dagger into her own chest.

CHAPTER FOURTEEN

*A*fter months holed up in Alister's library, Evelyn was nearly sick over the words she had translated. She had only finished half of the book, but what she had translated so far was terrible. The unnamed king was a monster.

She stood up and paced in front of the windows of the library. It was snowing. When had winter come? She wasn't cold. She looked around and noticed that a roaring fire was burning in a fireplace on the opposite side of the room. Who had been stoking it? She walked over to it and stabbed at the logs with a poker.

Alister was going to be so disappointed. She had been putting him off telling him parts of the story, saying that the story would make more sense the more she translated. But in truth, she had known for some time that the story was dark and frightening. She simply didn't know how to tell him that. They had both invested so much into the translation. It had been his father's prized possession. Surely Alister's father could not have known what the book contained. It was horrifying.

As a work of literature, she thought the book was fascinating. Like *Dracula* or *Frankenstein*. There was much to learn about human nature from the macabre. Yet she had hoped the book had contained much more than that. So much about the world had been discovered in books from the Near East. Many English scientists had built their knowledge of the universe, math, and science on the research discovered in Arabic texts. But this book would not be hailed as a great tome of learning.

Still, she had to tell Alister the truth. She could put it off no longer.

She gathered up the book and her notes and found him in one of the parlors, where he sat in front of the fire, drinking a brandy by the fire. She stopped to watch him for a moment. He was so handsome the way the fire reflected off his olive skin. And the way he thoughtfully read made her stomach quiver. Her one escape from the work had been their dinners together where he told her the news from the day or about a book he was reading. He knew she didn't have time to read for pleasure herself, so he summarized the books for her in animated fashion, as though she were watching a play as they ate their soup and chicken and enjoyed glasses of wine.

The small routine of life they had built together had been a true joy to her. She could happily continue on in such a manner. Her enjoying her work while he enjoyed the life of a country gentleman. The only thing she might change would be the scenery. She could easily continue her work while overlooking grape vineyards in Tuscany or sand dunes in Baghdad.

She also wouldn't object to a couple of children sitting by the fire as well, perhaps drawing or reading with their father as they waited for her to finish her tasks for the day. A dog by Alister's side certainly wouldn't go amiss either.

It was a pretty little life she imagined, but it would probably never come to pass. While she and Alister enjoyed their evenings together, her focus on her work had left room for little else. While Alister might steal the occasional kiss or touch, their relationship resembled nothing of a courtship. It was as though they were already an old married couple. Two people who enjoyed each other's company and lived under the same roof but led very separate lives devoid of affection.

What a dreadful thought.

She cleared her throat and stepped into the room. Alister immediately jumped to his feet and a smile spread across his face.

"So, the lady has emerged," he said.

"I...I have something to show you," she said, handing him the book and her notes.

"Do you dare let me read it?" he asked, his face brightening.

"It is time," she said. "It is not complete. I'm only about halfway through. But what I have seems to be a complete story."

"I can't wait to read it!" he said, taking the book and kissing her on the cheek. "Will you stay with me while I do so? In case I have questions along the way."

"Of course," Evelyn said as she poured herself a drink and sat in the chair opposite him by the fire. "I must warn you, though—"

"Oh no!" Alister said, interrupting her. "No warnings. You got to read it without any information beforehand. I want the same pleasure."

Evelyn pressed her lips but nodded. "Very well," she said as she took a long swig of her drink.

Alister settled himself comfortably in his chair and began to read. However, it did not take long for the smile to slowly leave his face.

"Oh...dear..." he mumbled several pages in. "Evelyn, are you...are you sure this is correct?"

"I am sure I have made some mistakes," she said. "But the essence of the story is sound."

He rubbed his chin as he kept reading.

Long into the night, they sat together, Alister's reactions often switching from surprise to disgust to shock. By the time he finished, Evelyn feared she was very nearly drunk.

"I...I can't believe what I just read," he finally said as he laid the book aside. "This must have been very difficult for you to translate."

"I admit that the little sleep I do get," Evelyn said, "is often...unsettled."

Alister stood and paced by the fire. "You must know I had no idea what the book entailed."

Evelyn chuckled. "How could you? No one in England could have read it before I came along."

"I just...I hope you don't think less of me for having you undertake such a horrid job," he said, kneeling before her and taking her hands in his.

"No," she said. "In spite of the book's terrible contents, I have never been happier in the past ten years than since I have been here working with you."

Alister smiled. "That does my heart glad." He then stood and resumed his pacing. "But that doesn't change my disappointment at knowing what the book contains. Or perhaps I should say *didn't* contain."

Evelyn sat quietly. She'd had months to consider the

content of the book; Alister only minutes. He needed time to process what he had read.

"My father, he was obsessed with this book," Alister went on. "He wanted nothing more than to read its words. But why? Did he have any idea what is was about? I wanted it translated in his honor because I thought it contained hidden knowledge. Something about science or math or the stars. But it is just a story about a monster. Nothing more than a worthless old wives' tale."

"Now, stop there," Evelyn said, standing. "Old wives' tales, folk tales, legends. They all have great value. They tell us about the people in a certain time and place. What they believed. What they feared. What they loved. And when we read these stories, our reactions to them tell us about ourselves as well."

"That might be true," Alister said. "But this cannot be what my father thought it would contain."

Evelyn shrugged. "Does it matter?" she asked. "We can't change what is written here. The book is a tale of an evil, insane king. That's a fact. All we can do is accept that and appreciate it for what it is. Wishing it were something else will not change that."

Alister smirked and walked over to her. He rubbed her arms and then hugged her tight. She wrapped her arms around him and laid her head on his chest. He was warm and smelled of musk and spice.

"Your optimism surprises me," he said. "You have dedicated so much to this book. Staked your entire career on it."

"I could still have a fabulous career," she said. "If 'The Cask of Amontillado' can find fame I am sure a story as wicked as this one can too."

Alister laughed. "You are a fan of Poe, are you?"

"He is a brilliant example of being able to find the beauty of life in even its ugliest moments," she said.

"So," Alister said, returning to the book. "What are we to do now?"

"That's up to you," Evelyn said. "You are the patron and the book's owner."

"Would you think me insane if I asked you to continue?" Alister asked.

"Would you think me insane if I wanted to continue?" Evelyn replied. "We've come this far. I think we should see it through."

"Agreed," Alister said. "However…" He walked over and retrieved the newspaper he was reading earlier. "I demand you take a night off. There is an event tomorrow evening at the museum. A celebration of Sumerian language and culture."

"Are you serious?" Evelyn asked, taking the paper from him and reading the announcement. "To highlight the museum's extensive collection and recognize the great achievements of the museum's researchers in history and linguistics." She threw the paper aside and crossed her arms in a huff. "Linguistics!"

Alister laughed. "Can you imagine how paltry their translations must be when compared to yours?"

"Henry Wilkes wishes he could translate something as complicated as a vase," Evelyn said. "But the most he could ever accomplish would be 'See Jane Run.' You cannot think I would enjoy returning there after the way he treated me."

Alister shrugged. "It might be a good opportunity to share some of the strides you've made," he said. "Take some of your notes. I could talk about how brilliant you are. I know the book is far from complete, but it might do some good to get people talking about you and the discovery of the new language now. Then when you are ready to go public, the people will be dying for more information."

"Have you ever worked in publicity, Mr. Shaw?" Evelyn asked, her eyebrow raised.

"I do know how to get attention when I want it," he said.

Evelyn picked the newspaper up again. "I can't imagine that Henry will be happy to see me. We did not leave on good terms."

Alister pulled the newspaper out of her hands. "Forget Henry Wilkes," he said. Then he placed a finger on her lips. "I don't want to hear of that man vexing you ever again."

Evelyn's breathing quickened and her heart raced. She had been so lost in her work, she had forgotten what it was like to be touched by this man. She would need to give him far more of her attention.

"Henry...who?" she asked breathlessly.

Alister pulled her to him tightly and placed his lips on hers. "Oh, how I have missed you, my pet," he whispered in her ear.

"And I you," Evelyn replied.

"Perhaps," Alister managed to say between kissed, "tomorrow night, we could attend the event not as an employee and employer, but as a man and woman who can't take their eyes off each other."

Evelyn pulled away, her eyes open in shock. "Alister," she gasped. "Are you saying what I think you are saying?"

He took her hand and pulled her back into his embrace. "Evelyn Crowley," he said, "will you permit me to court you?"

"Oh, Alister!" she cried. "Yes! Yes!"

She jumped up to her tiptoes to return her lips to his. He laughed as they kissed, their hands running wild.

"I fear, my darling," Alister said, "that it will be nearly impossible to keep your virtue intact for much longer."

Evelyn nodded. "I know the feeling," she said. "We will have to be careful. We should inform Susan and Mrs. Paxton of the change in our circumstances so they can serve as suitable chaperones."

"I am afraid I don't know the rules in this situation," he said. "If you had a father, I'd request permission to marry you tomorrow."

"I fear that for us, there are no rules," she said. "We have no family and few friends. Who would there even be a wedding for?"

"Are you suggesting that we elope?" Alister asked her, his eyes wild.

Evelyn pulled away from him, gasping for breath and a moment to collect her thoughts. She had never even considered something so brazen. So contrary to polite society. But then, why not?

Still, she pulled away until they were no longer touching. "I...I can't think straight," she said. "I believe passion has gotten the better of our good senses."

"I think I prefer passion to good sense," Alister said.

"I never thought I would say it," Evelyn said with a nod, "but I do too."

Alister took a step forward to embrace her again, but she held up her hand.

"Still, cooler heads must prevail," she said. "I...I do not want to do something we will regret."

"If you walk away from me now," Alister said, taking a step forward and looking at her with heavy-lidded eyes. "You might find you regret it when you are trying to fall asleep in your cold and empty bed."

"Perhaps," Evelyn acquiesced. "But we have the rest of our lives to make up for that."

Alister laughed. "I can't argue with that. Go. Retreat back to your library or your room before I change my mind and ravage you right here."

"Don't tempt me to stay," Evelyn said as she grabbed the book and held it in front of her like a shield as she backed out of the room. She heard Alister laugh again as she safely exited the room and let the door close behind her.

She couldn't believe what just happened. She, Evelyn Crowley, was being courted by the man of her dreams.

CHAPTER FIFTEEN

"Your knee is shaking the whole carriage," Alister said. He gently placed his hand on Evelyn's leg, which made her heart beat even faster.

"I'm sorry," she said as she tried to will herself to calm down. "I don't know why I am so nervous." She started to chew on her thumbnail, but Alister reached over and took her hand in his. She looked down at their intertwined fingers. She knew she should pull her hand away, but she didn't want to. His touch both thrilled her and calmed her. She felt that with him by her side, she could do anything.

"You are just worried about seeing that dreadful Henry Wilkes again," Alister said.

"I hope you are not jealous," Evelyn said.

Alister let out a full, hearty laugh. "Jealous? Why would I be jealous? He's a pompous little windbag who cannot hold a candle to your intellect. I'd be more jealous of that little cat you have been spoiling."

Evelyn laughed as well. It was true that she had grown rather fond of Susan's kitten, who had grown quite fat since they took her in. The kitten seemed to think she had two mothers, spending her time equally between Susan and Evelyn.

"I suppose I am just worried about what Henry has in store for tonight," Evelyn said as she looked out the window of the carriage. It was already dark out. It was late December, so evenings came early, along with a bitter chill and snow often. "We did not leave on very good terms. Then, he arranges a Sumerian celebration and doesn't invite me? I feel almost as though he is taking a personal stab at me."

"He probably is," Alister said. "Small men are often petty. And after your last encounter, he probably knew that you would never come back. He has to show the museum directors that he knows what he is doing without you there to do the work for him."

"Do you think he will be angry I showed up?" Evelyn asked.

"Yes," Alister said. Evelyn looked at him with a grimace, suddenly doubting their decision to attend. "But that will just make the evening all the more enjoyable for me."

"As long as you have a good time, I suppose that is the most important thing," Evelyn teased.

Alister laughed and kissed the top of her head. "Fear not, my darling. I'm sure you will have a lovely evening as well."

They arrived a few minutes late. With the slush on the roads, traveling through London's busy streets was more treacherous than usual and the carriage driver had to be extra cautious.

Evelyn and Alister stepped inside the large front doors of the building and a butler took their coats and other winter sundry. By the warm light of the electric lamps, the interior of the museum took on a golden glow. Evelyn had to catch her breath at the beauty of it, the various exhibits gleaming behind glass. The main hall was nearly empty except for a few people milling about. But she could hear Henry's voice echoing from the Sumerian exhibit hall upstairs. He apparently made some sort of joke that caused the room to break out into laughter.

Evelyn paused and put her hand to her chest. She was still doubting if she should have come. She appreciated Alister's support, but she wasn't used to confrontation.

Alister took her hand and brought it to his lips. "Come," he said, gently pulling her toward the stairs. She followed. She would follow him anywhere.

"The museum could not be more proud of the advances we have made in Sumerian translation over the years," she could hear Henry say. "But especially the progress made over the last few months."

Few months? Evelyn wondered. Had the museum hired new translators since she was last here? Of course, to many people, even Henry's rudimentary translation skills were impressive.

"Truly, we are on the cusp of a new Renaissance," Henry went on as Evelyn reached the second floor and walked toward his voice. "One where all the hidden knowledge of the Orient is at our fingertips."

Evelyn suddenly had a sinking feeling in her stomach. What was he talking about?

"Through the discovery of new models of translation," Henry said, "the Sumerian language is no longer a mystical secret, but merely a complicated puzzle we are on the cusp of deciphering."

By the time Evelyn walked into the room, her heart was in her nose. She knew that she should leave. That whatever Henry said next was going to be devastating, but she pressed forward. She had to face what was coming.

"Behold!" Henry said, pulling a cord that released a curtain that revealed the vase and a large display explaining the fundamentals of archaic Sumerian. "The secrets of Sumerian explained!"

The crowd gasped and then clapped. Evelyn clenched her jaw tightly and squeezed Alister's hand so tightly he winced.

"What's wrong?" Alister whispered, but Evelyn was seething so hard her vision was turning red.

"What exactly does this mean?" one of the women in the audience asked as everyone gathered around the vase to get a better look.

"Are you familiar with the Rosetta Stone?" Henry asked. "This vase, this Persian Pot, is the same thing, but for Sumerian. By translating the archaic Sumerian into a more modern version and then to English, we can make complete sense of the old language."

"Can you read it?" a man asked.

Henry laughed. "Not quite yet. But it is only a matter of time. I have some of the best minds in the world working on a cipher as we speak."

"So *you* are not able to translate it?" someone else asked.

Henry chuffed at that a bit. "Translation has always been a multi-layered field. But it was my initial discovery of the vase and the first few connections that paved the way for a full translation. Typically, such a deciphering of a new language would take years. But based on my initial research, and now with the help of other experts from around the globe, we should have a full working dictionary in only a few months."

"You jerk!" Evelyn exclaimed, unable to control herself any longer. The whole crowd turned and looked at her, but she didn't care. "You stole my research!"

The crowd then gasped and turned back to Henry. "Evelyn!" he stammered. "What are you doing here?"

She stepped toward him, the crowd parting to let her through as they watched with fascination. No doubt they thought they were about to get a good show.

"Now, Evelyn," Henry said. "Let's talk about this rationally."

"I am rational!" Evelyn exclaimed. "That's why you didn't invite me to the event. You didn't want me to know that you'd stolen my work and sent it out without my knowledge or permission."

"I didn't invite you because I didn't think you would want to come," Henry said. "The last time you were here, you stormed out in a fit of anger, similar to now."

"Because you wouldn't give me a job," she said.

"A job?" Henry asked with a guffaw. "You aren't an archeologist or a linguist. You haven't been to university."

"I have far more experience—" she started to say, but Henry interrupted her.

"You are just a hobbyist whom I entertained for far too long," Henry said, finding his courage as he looked around to the other men in the room. "This is what happens when we let women spend too much time out of the home." The men in the room laughed, except for Alister, the rage on his face matching Evelyn's.

"You will watch your tongue when you speak to a lady, *Mr.* Wilkes," Alister growled, reminding Henry of his station. The smug smile fled from Henry's face. It was a low blow that Evelyn wouldn't have taken herself—she wanted recognition on her merit, not her title—but she appreciated that Henry had been silenced for a moment. She placed her hand on Alister's arm and stepped from his side to in front of him. She was grateful for his support, but she needed to defend herself.

"I am *not* a mere hobbyist," she said. "Those translation notes..." She pointed to the display behind the vase. "Those are mine. The last time I was here, I dropped my papers. Did you steal some of them?"

Henry scoffed. "You can't prove those are your notes," he said. "I made the discovery, as the head of the Sumerian department."

"I can confirm that Henry came to me months ago with this information," one of the museum directors said, stepping forward. "He was quite excited about what he had found."

"I'm sure he was," Evelyn said. "But did you ask him to explain them to you?"

"Why would I?" the man said. "I can't make heads or tails of it."

"But there are ways to explain translation to laypersons," Evelyn said. "None of you can read ancient Egyptian either, yet you trust your translators to explain it."

"Yes," the man said. "But we know several people who can read Egyptian nowadays. No one here reads Sumerian. Until we hear back from the other experts—"

"I can," Evelyn said. "I can read high Sumerian. And I can make some sense of archaic Sumerian now because of the work I have been doing for Lord Craven."

"You mean the man you are living with?" Henry jibbed, and the room gasped. Evelyn felt her face go hot. Even though she had nothing to be embarrassed about, the insinuation stung. And the accusation in public was sure to hurt her reputation, not matter how baseless.

"How dare you!" Evelyn snapped. "Lord Craven is my

patron. I am working for him to translate a book. There is nothing untoward in it and I demand an apology."

"You storm in here," Henry said, "interrupting my event, making false accusations of your own against my work and character, and then have the gall to demand an apology from me? Madam, you have certainly gone too far!"

Several people in the room began to murmur, shaking their heads and tsking their tongues.

"I do believe, Lady Sommers," another museum director said, stepping forward, "you have made enough of a scene this evening."

"I am not making a scene," Evelyn said. "I only want proper credit for the work I have done. If you will just let me show you my notes from the translations I've already done, I think you'll see—"

The man held up his hand and motioned toward the door. "As Mr. Wilkes has already explained, we have several real experts from around the globe already working on a proper translation."

Evelyn's heart sank. It was all over. No one would ever believe that she had made the discovery and completed the first translations. With other translations now using her initial notes, they would surely be able to come to an understanding of Sumerian soon, without her help. Henry would get the credit for planting the seeds of understanding. He was right—she couldn't prove that the notes were hers first. There was no way to prove her dates were correct. He could simply continue to say that the notes were originally his and no one could correct him. Since she had done the work alone, she had no one to corroborate her story. Alister knew the truth, but he wasn't a respected voice in historical circles. And Henry—with a single sentence—had cast doubt on the professional nature of their relationship. No, there was nothing Evelyn could do to prove that Henry had stolen her work.

Evelyn held her chin up and turned toward the door, walking out with her head held high, even as she was falling apart inside.

"Evelyn," Alister whispered harshly as he followed, obviously wanting her to continue to fight back, but she held up her hand to silence him as she walked toward the front door. She knew she couldn't speak. If she tried to speak, she would cry. And she refused to cry in front of these men. Especially Henry. He might have won, but she would not let him know that she had been utterly defeated.

Evelyn and Alister collected their things and then climbed into the carriage. They rode in silence, Evelyn staring out the window as her emotions swayed back and forth from despair to anger and back again.

"I'm sorry," Alister finally said as they neared his estate. "I should not have pressured you into attending."

"It is not your fault," Evelyn managed to say as she ran her gloved hand over the satin of her skirt. "It had already been done. Henry had taken the credit and sent the work out to other translators. It might be for the best that I found out tonight. Had I sent the work out later without knowing, I would have looked a fool."

"Are you sure there is nothing you can do to prove that you were the person who made the first translation?" Alister asked. "I'll support anything you say."

Evelyn shook her head. "I'll be nothing more than a footnote in history," she said. "A woman with a brilliant understanding of language, but who only stood on the research of those men who came before her."

Alister hit the carriage door with his fist. "It's not right!"

"It is what it is," Evelyn said calmly. "I'm not the first

woman to have her work stolen by a man."

"What do you mean?" Alister asked.

"Have you heard of Charles Babbage?" she asked.

"The mathematician?" Alister said. "Of course."

"Have you heard of Ada Lovelace?"

"Lord Byron's daughter? A rather scandalous girl, wasn't she?"

"She designed Babbage's analytical machine," Evelyn said.

Alister laughed, but when he saw the serious look Evelyn shot him, he stopped abruptly. "What? You must be joking."

Evelyn blew out an annoyed breath and turned to the window again. "You doubt it is possible after what you just witnessed tonight?"

"I...I'm sorry," Alister stammered. "You are right. It should not surprise me, but I suppose I'm still in shock."

"It's not your fault," Evelyn said. "Life is just so easy for you."

"Should I apologize for that?" Alister said, chuffing a bit.

"No," Evelyn said. "Simply have more empathy for me, and every woman relegated to the home when our brains are capable of so much more."

Alister reached over and took her hand, kissing it again. "I will do my best."

Evelyn looked over and gave him a small smile, which was the most she could muster. She appreciated his willingness to listen, but she was exhausted, mentally and emotionally. When they arrived at the house, she couldn't bear to enter her study. Instead, she climbed the stairs to her room.

She called for Susan, but she fell asleep before Susan could appear.

CHAPTER SIXTEEN

*E*velyn was awakened to the sound of the cat mewling loudly. She groaned and rolled over. Her head felt like it had been rolled over by a truck. The cat continued to meow. Evelyn threw one of her pillows at her, but the kitten seemed to take that as an invitation to jump onto the bed and onto Evelyn's back—and continue her incessant cawing.

"Oh, do stop!" Evelyn said, swinging her arm around, which the cat deftly avoided, only to then get into Evelyn's face and purr.

"The one day I decide to avoid getting out of bed and you choose to bother me instead of Susan," Evelyn said in annoyance, but she couldn't resist reaching out and petting the cat's soft fur. It was then that she remembered that Susan didn't appear last night either. She sat up and looked around the room. Her clothes were still on the floor, so Susan had not been here the night before or this morning. Where was she?

Evelyn pulled her covers back and instantly regretted it,

quickly pulling her warm blanket back over her. The fire had gone out and the room was freezing.

"Susan!" Evelyn called out as she rummaged in a nearby drawer for some woolen socks, but Susan did not come.

"What day is it?" Evelyn asked the kitten, who paced by her empty food bowl. She supposed it could have been Susan's day off. All the days blended together and it was easy for her to lose track. Still, it wasn't like Susan to be gone overnight. She racked her brain, trying to remember if Susan had mentioned going to visit her family or beau, but she couldn't recall any such conversation. But Susan was a grown woman, free to come and go as she pleased. Evelyn was sure she would have a good explanation for her sudden disappearance when she returned. No reason to be concerned just yet.

Evelyn dressed herself and then went downstairs to the kitchen where the cook and Mrs. Paxton were having tea. They both leaped to their feet when Evelyn entered.

"Forgive me," Evelyn said. "But I think it must be Susan's day off. Can someone please stoke the fire in my room and take up some food for the cat."

"Of course, ma'am," Mrs. Paxton said and then started to say something else, but hesitated.

"Something on your mind?" Evelyn prodded.

"It's just...well, I wasn't informed that today was the girl's day off. I'm supposed to be kept abreast of such things as head of the staff."

Evelyn nodded to hide her grimace. Mrs. Paxton was partially right. Susan did usually report to her, but only in the interest of keeping the peace. Susan wasn't really under the housekeeper's purview since she worked for Evelyn and not Alister. But Evelyn knew her annoyance truly laid with

Henry, not Mrs. Paxton, so she took a calming breath and held her tongue.

"I'm sorry for the inconvenience," Evelyn finally said. "I hope the extra work won't be a problem for you."

Mrs. Paxton tilted her head and looked down her nose at Evelyn, as though she had won some great debate. "No, it's no trouble, ma'am. Do you require anything else?"

"No, thank you," Evelyn said and quickly left the room before she let fly words she couldn't easily take back. She paused before heading upstairs, though. She knew she should head to the library, but she was dreading it. After the events of last night, the excitement over her work had significantly waned. But she couldn't go back to her cold room, and she wasn't ready to face Alistair. As well-intentioned as he was, she wasn't in the mood to discuss the previous night. She finally took a deep breath and forced one foot in front of the other down the hall toward the library.

It seemed strange to her upon entering how nothing seemed to have changed. The room was warm and inviting, the curtains pulled back to allow in plenty of light, the smell of the old books was as delicious as a fresh pastry. For some reason, she thought the room would be somehow... different after the event at the museum. She felt different enough. No longer did she feel confident in her abilities, excited to get to work, and hopeful of the future. It was almost an insult that the room should maintain its sense of welcoming cheer when she couldn't have felt more despondent. It would have been nice if the library had the decency to match her mood, but she knew that was far too much to ask of a room.

She crossed over to her desk and looked down at the book that was supposed to be her magnum opus. Her great work. The book that was supposed to change her life. It took all her self-control to not fling it into the fire and be done with it. Not that it would change anything except cause more pain. Alister would never forgive her. She instantly regretted the impulse. He had been right about one thing, she could still translate the book and be a proper translator in her own right, even if she wouldn't be known as the person who deciphered the language. She could still receive her laurels. But part of her would always know—it could have been more.

She cleared her throat and sat down to work and realized that the book was open to a page she had not been working on previously. It was open very near the back. She looked around the desk and saw that many of her notes were also scattered about. She quickly rifled through them, terrified that Henry might have somehow gained access to the room and stolen some more of her notes, but she didn't think any of them were missing. Still, something wasn't right. Someone had been here.

She opened her mouth to call for Susan, but then shut it, remembering that the girl was out. She felt a small flutter of anxiety in her chest. Even though Susan didn't have to report to Mrs. Paxton, it *was* odd that she had not. She was now sure that Susan had not mentioned leaving town to her either. Well, no sense in panicking just yet. She'd only been gone a few hours. If she weren't back by evening, she would talk to Alister about sending for the police.

She decided to get to work on the page the book was open to. It seemed as good a place to start as any. At first, it was hard to get started. She didn't have Susan to bring her tea and she was certain she had not laced her corset up correctly as it seemed to pinch her in all the wrong places, but after a while, she got back into the rhythm of her work and made some progress.

After a few hours, though, she was surprised by what she was reading. It appeared to be the instructions the enchantress followed to make the evil king immortal. There was a list of ingredients, flowers and oils and even the dried corpse of a desert rat known as a jerboa. There were instructions for where to stand under a full moon and certain movements of the feet and hands. Finally, there was mention of slaying a child and imbibing the blood.

Her hands started to shake so violently she had to drop her pen and walk away from the book. She wasn't sure why what she had read affected her so. It was just a story. A wildly frightening and disturbing story, but a fiction nonetheless.

Right?

But then why was the spell included? And in such detail. She had never seen such a thing before.

She decided that she needed to tell Alister what she had discovered. She didn't know what he would think of it, but she needed to tell someone, unburden herself of the knowledge. She stuck her head into the hallway and called his name. He appeared only a moment later.

"Evelyn," he said, a wide smile on his face. He took her hands in his and squeezed them, but he did not try to kiss her. Perhaps he knew she was not in the mood for lovemaking. "How are you, my dear?"

"Shaken," she said plainly, leading him into the room. "I have translated something I think you should see."

"Oh, I am so glad you decided to return to work today," he said. "I was worried you might abandon the project—and me—altogether after last night."

Evelyn paused, debating if she should tell him the truth.

But she decided it was best if there were no secrets between them.

"I...I was tempted to give up," she said. "I didn't even want to get out of bed this morning. But dear Susan's cat wouldn't let me sleep, so why not continue the work? What else do I have to fill my time?"

Alister smirked and opened his mouth to say something, but then quickly shut it. Evelyn cocked an eyebrow, sure he had planned to say something wildly inappropriate but then thought better of it.

"So," he said, apparently deciding to focus on the work at hand. "What did you want to show me?"

"I think it is the magic spell the enchantress used to make the evil king immortal," she said, hardly believing the words that were coming out of her mouth. It was ludicrous!

Alister chuckled, then looked at her notes and the book itself, and he realized she was serious. "This...this is truly shocking," he finally said.

"I know," she replied, standing next to him. "But I can provide no other explanation for what is written here."

"So this is why he..." Alister started to say, but then he ran his hand over his mouth.

"Who?" Evelyn asked. "What?"

"My father," he said, unable to tear his eyes away from the book. "Why he wanted the book translated."

Evelyn was still confused. "You mean when he was alive?"

"What?" Alister said, looking up at her, worry on his face and his eyes red around the edges. "Oh, yes. As you say." He turned back to the book and started flipping the pages as though he could make any sense of it.

"What are you looking for?" she asked. "What's wrong?"

"Is there anything here about ending the enchantment?"

he asked. "Or more information about the curse itself? The terms or...or loopholes to end it?"

"Umm..." Evelyn thought those were strange things to ask. "I...I don't know. I have shown you everything I have translated so far, but there is still more to the book. But what does it matter? None of it is real. It's just a story. A fantasy."

Alister looked at her as though she had slapped him, hurt and confusion rippling across his face. He quickly crossed the room toward the door.

"Of course," he said.

"Where are you going?" she asked, worried she had offended him somehow.

"I just need to check something," he said. "Stay here and lock the door. And keep working on the translation."

He left the room, slamming the door behind him.

Evelyn felt a cold chill wash over her that had nothing to do with the temperature of the room.

CHAPTER SEVENTEEN

ock the door? Evelyn wondered as she walked back to her desk. Why would she need to lock the door? Only she, Alister, and the servants were home. But something about the book had clearly unnerved Alister. But what? And what was that about the spell being why his father wanted the book translated? His father was dead.

Evelyn shook her head and sat at the desk once again. There was nothing more she could do about Alister and his strange behavior right now. She would have to wait to prod him for more information when he returned. She turned the page and continued working.

The book went on to explain some of the finer points about how the enchantment had worked. The enchantress had told the queen that the king's body would rot, but his soul would remain. The queen had thought this a fitting punishment, for him to live forever in a useless hollow shell. But apparently, the enchantress had not been completely honest with the queen. The king's soul was not trapped in his mortal body, but was able to leap from one person to another, thus living forever.

Evelyn sat back and shuddered at the thought. How terrifying! To one moment be yourself, and the next, to completely overtaken by a monster. Not for the first time, she was glad the book was fiction. She was riveted, though. Why would the enchantress lie to the queen like that? Why would she want the king to live forever? He was evil!

The book went on to say that the enchantress had hoped that the king would reward her for saving his life, but he killed her instead. He then vowed to never give up his quest for true immortality, one that would allow him to stay in one body for all of time.

I, Agga-Namzu, loyal servant of the High Priestess Belit-Sheri, She of the Moon and Stars, have written a full and true account of the life and deeds of King Dagon, a most evil and wicked ruler, that others may know the cost of such power and unnatural desire. As of now, I do not know where King Dagon's soul has fled. When She of the Moon and Stars refused to complete the enchantment to make the king a True Immortal, he slayed her with her own dagger. But with her dying breath, she left a final enchantment in the world. If a person stabs King Dagon in the heart with the dagger and recites the words below, his body and immortal soul will finally perish. May She of the Moon and Stars guide my hand and whoever reads these words, so that Evil may be destroyed and peace return to the world.

What then followed was something very difficult to translate. The words came slowly, but she couldn't decipher the meaning. She finally realized that it was written in verse, like a poem. Poetry translation was a completely different level of interpretation. But why would a poem be included? She wanted to dismiss the idea, but couldn't ignore the thought that she was reading a magic spell, one that would end the evil king for good.

Evelyn leaned back and pondered over what she had

just read. The book had been written by one of the enchantress's acolytes after the evil king killed her. Though, Evelyn rather thought the enchantress had it coming. She was the one who gave the king immortality in the first place. She had ordered him to kill his infant son. It was she who then deceived the queen and allowed the king to keep living by jumping from body to body for all of time. The enchantress clearly had her own agenda, her own wicked desires in mind when she allowed all this to happen.

Evelyn sat back up and laughed at herself at how seriously she was taking all this. It was just a story! Wasn't it?

She stood and stretched her back and looked around the room. It was bright, but not by light from the windows, but the lamps. She did briefly recall Mrs. Paxton stepping into the room. She must have come in and turned on the lights as the sun started to set.

Had the sun set?

She rushed to the window and looked out. It was pitch black! What time was it? Where was Alister? And Susan! Susan never returned. Panic swelled in her chest and this time, she could not quell it. Something was terribly wrong. She needed to find Alister and alert the police immediately.

Evelyn stepped out into the hallway and called for Alister. This time, though, he did not appear.

"Mrs. Paxton!" she tried instead as she made her way to the main entry hall. Still, there was no reply. There was not a maid or footman to be seen. *Where was everyone?*

"I'm just...scaring myself," she said out loud to try and calm her nerves as she rubbed her arms with her hands. "That stupid book is just making me jump as shadows."

But she knew she wasn't imagining the fact that she was alone in the house. That Alister had fled suddenly. That Susan was missing.

Her eyes jumped up to the third-floor gallery when she thought she heard a creaking sound, like that of a door slowly opening. She held her breath, expecting to see someone appear. But no one did. She did see a light coming from down the third-floor hall, though, near the rooms where Alister kept his father's treasures. She licked her dry lips and slowly began to make her way upstairs toward the light. She gripped the handrail as she ascended, her eyes wide open for any movement.

"Alister?" she called out as she made it to the third floor. "Mrs. Paxton?"

There was no reply. The light was coming from the room where Alister had gathered all of his father's Sumerian artifacts. Had Alister been looking for something in that room? She crept toward the room.

"Alister?" she said, her voice nearly a quaking whisper as she slowly pushed the door open.

No one was there.

She exhaled a sigh of relief, though she wasn't exactly sure why. What did she think she was going to find in here? An evil immortal king waiting to jump into her body? She nearly laughed out loud.

A cold breeze caressed her face. She looked across the room and saw that the window to the room was open. She grimaced. That was not good. The cold and damp could damage the artifacts. She had no desire to go into the room, but the historian in her couldn't allow the artifacts to be exposed to the elements for even a moment. She rushed across the room to the window.

The wind had blown the window completely open, and the pane banged against the side of the house. Evelyn had to lean out the window, standing on her tiptoes to reach it. She finally managed to grip it and pull it closed so it latched tightly. But as she leaned back inside, she lost her balance and fell to the side, knocking over a stack of unlabeled boxes.

She gasped when she saw a familiar face looking back at her. There on the wall, behind where the boxes once stood, was the portrait of a man she had long forgotten. Along with her very painful memories.

Suddenly, she was a girl again, on a hot summer day in Persia. Her father had decided to take her with him to the dig site. A rare treat indeed! Her dear friend Hamid was there as well. She had missed him and their language lessons so.

But as she approached the entrance to the excavation pit, a man was there to greet her. A lord, but one she had not met before. She didn't know his name at the time. She didn't think it was important.

But now here he was, standing right in front of her!

She placed her hand on her chest to calm her rapidly beating heart as she leaned forward to read the name under the portrait.

Bannister Shaw, Lord Craven.

Of course! Her father had called the man "Ol' Banning!" She had blocked the horrible memories of that day out, including meeting the old Lord Craven, Alister's father. He *had* been there that day! But why wasn't he in any of the news reports or pictures? Even if he hadn't been an official member of the expedition, he should have been listed among the dead...

Except he didn't die that day! According to Alister, his father had only died recently. So there had been two survivors of the sandstorm that day—Evelyn Crowley and Bannister Shaw!

But...how? And why was she not told of this before?

Why didn't anyone seem to know this? She began to pace and found it hard to breathe. She was on the cusp of learning something she wasn't sure she wanted to learn. But she couldn't stop herself. Once the floodgates of her memories were open, she could not close them.

She remembered that her father and the other lords had brought her to the dig site to translate something. Out of all those so-called educated men, they had needed her—a little girl—to read a book to them.

A book! She had been tasked with reading a book. But not just *a* book—*the* book. The very book she had been translating for Alister. She now knew she had seen it before, on the day her father died. No wonder it felt familiar to her but she didn't recognize it. She had completely blocked out any memory of that fateful day.

But now, everything was coming back to her, and everything was connected. Somehow. She wasn't sure what was going on, but it could not be a coincidence that she and Bannister Shaw had both survived the accident and that she had now been tasked with translating the book.

A book that led to her father's death. A book that changed Bannister Shaw for the worse. A book that now was throwing her life into turmoil. When she had first read from the book all those years ago, did she unwittingly release something? Something...*utuk xul*? Something evil?

And what did Alister know?

She was a fool. She had been far too trusting of that handsome, charismatic man. She had begun to love him! Idiot!

She continued to pace. She needed to puzzle this out as much as possible before confronting Alister. What did all this mean? Somehow, Bannister Shaw survived the accident, took the book, and hid it away here at Carnarvon

Castle. Nearly a decade later, Bannister died, and his son, Alister, hired Evelyn to translate the book—Bannister's prized possession—in his father's honor.

She started to calm down. There was perhaps nothing nefarious in it after all. There could be a perfectly reasonable explanation for why Lord Craven's presence at the site that day had been kept a secret. She just couldn't think of any at the moment. Her mind was racing wildly, but she was still having trouble thinking straight. But maybe Alister would know why. He did know that his father had been in Persia around the time of the accident. He had already admitted that much. Perhaps he knew more than even he realized. After all, he had not been close to his father.

She needed to find Alister. He would have the answers to all this, she was sure of it.

She started to leave the room, determined to find out where Alister had gone, when she began to hear the low droning sound once again. The sound of many people chanting. And it was growing louder.

Evelyn rushed back to the window and looked out it. From this higher vantage point, she could definitely make out a red glowing light in the distance. The chanting was coming from the same direction.

She nearly flew out of the room and down the stairs. She grabbed her cloak from a hook by the door and went out into the cold, dark night. She ran toward the light, the chanting growing louder. She had forgotten what lay in the direction she was headed in until she saw it—Lord Craven's Crypt.

She gasped when she saw that the bright red light was emanating from the crypt itself.

CHAPTER EIGHTEEN

*E*ven though she had been here before, the crypt now was much more frightening. Imposing. Haunting. The chanting was so loud, it was as though she was surrounded by people, yet she was alone. The chanting was coming from inside the crypt—a crypt that was emitting a red light.

She could feel in her bones that danger was here. That book, it was more than just a story. She knew that now. But even if the tale of the evil king had only been allegory or exaggeration, for her personally, the book was a curse. The last time she saw it, dozens of people—including her own father—died. Now, who knew what strange thing was happening inside the crypt. The chanting, perhaps some sort of cultist ritual? It sounded crazy, but she had heard stories of such things happening. Cults, witches, and neo-pagans preforming rituals and sacrifices in the name of whatever religion or deity was the current fad. Such stories always made for an entertaining read in newspapers and Penny Dreadfuls. But that she should be face to face with something so...so unbelievable was impossible to ignore.

She knew she should get help. But from where? She couldn't find any of the servants to saddle a horse or prepare a carriage. She was miles from town. And Alister wasn't anywhere to be found. No, she needed to find out what was going on and try to stop it herself.

She pushed on the large stone slab that covered the entrance to the crypt, but it didn't budge an inch. She ran her hands all over the front of the slab and the stone walls around it, searching for a switch or lever of some sort, but she found nothing. She grunted in annoyance and kicked the slab, which she instantly regretted as she grabbed the toe of her foot in pain.

She looked at the words over the door. In addition to Bannister Shaw's name, there were archaic Sumerian symbols. While they didn't make sense to her before, she could now read them. She didn't quite understand the meaning, but she could speak the words.

"*Qabû mutu u sar*," she said, and to her surprise, the stone slab moved! She jumped back as the slab rumbled and shifted to the side. Hot air puffed into her face, blowing her hair back and the chanting grew even louder. She stepped inside the crypt and it was so hot, she had to remove her cloak, which she laid just inside the door.

The crypt was not really a crypt—there was no coffin or shelves for corpses. Instead, there was only a stairwell that led deep underground. She slowly and carefully descended the stairs.

The stairwell eventually opened into a large antechamber lit with dozens of torches and braziers that were causing the reddish light and the heat. There were countless people in dark robes standing around, including all of the household staff! She could clearly see Mrs. Paxton, the cook, and the carriage driver. She had no idea who many of the other people were, though.

On the ground very near her, she saw Alister. He was trussed like a turkey with his hands tied behind his back and a gag tied around his mouth. He rolled to one side and looked dazed, a black and blue bruise forming on his forehead. Someone had given him a nasty blow. She had to fight the urge to run to him. These were clearly dangerous people. She had to be careful.

She moved along the wall, staying behind large stones and slabs, to get a better look at what all the cultists seemed to be looking at in the middle of the room. Finally, she caught a glimpse of Susan! She was tied to a stone slab in the middle of the room wearing only her white cotton nightgown.

Evelyn felt a pang of guilt. She knew something was wrong! Yet she had ignored the signs and left Susan here to who knew what abuses from these deranged people! She had to help her.

But on the other side of Susan was a man she never expected to see.

Lord Craven. Bannister Shaw himself.

He was alive! And he seemed to be presiding over the macabre ritual in his purple robes with his hands held aloft as he looked up at the ceiling. Seeing his face again, after so many years, sent a chill straight into Evelyn's heart.

He stood over Susan with an ornate, curved dagger in his hand. Evelyn immediately thought of the dagger mentioned in the book. Could it possibly be the same one? Lord Craven ran his hand through Susan's hair, and she tried to recoil from his touch but was tied fast.

"Blessed girl," Lord Craven said, his deep voice carrying through the room and reverberating off the stone walls.

"Virgin maid. Vessel for my seed. Incubator for my progeny. Through you, I shall live for time immemorial!"

Susan screamed and cried. "Don't you dare touch me, you old goat!"

Lord Craven just laughed.

Evelyn felt sick to her stomach. Lord Craven either was or at least thought he was the spirit of the evil king! He wanted to impregnate Susan and then kill their child. He must have thought that by completing the ceremony again it would make him truly immortal.

Alister must have come to at some point because he now attempted to yell at his father through his muffling gag. Lord Craven looked at him.

"And you, my son," Lord Craven said. "My first-born. You shall be the new home for my soul. I could not live forever as an old man. What is the point of that? But you, young and strong, I will give you the ultimate gift! My immortal soul!"

So, Alister was only a pawn as well. Old Lord Craven was going to leap into Alister's body just before completing the ceremony in the hopes of living forever as a young man. The old king was truly evil! He had to be stopped!

Lord Craven turned away from Alister and Susan and raised his eyes and hands toward a relief carving of a woman in a flowing dress surrounded by stars and the moon.

"High Priestess," Lord Craven said. "She of the Moon and Stars, hear me! Bless this dagger and my seed! Bring me a new child. One worthy of my strength and power!"

Evelyn took the opportunity to climb out from behind her rock and go to Alister's side.

"Shh!" she said before he even saw her so he wouldn't make a noise.

He looked up at her, his eyes wide, shocked to see her. But he nodded his understanding.

Evelyn undid the gag around his mouth and saw blood on it. He had taken quite a beating. She then worked on untying his hands. Once his hands were free, he could not resist grabbing her head and kissing her, only for a moment.

"We have to get out of here!" he then whispered as he worked to untie his feet. "We can go for the police and—"

"Not without Susan!" she interrupted.

"We can come back for her," he said, tossing the bounds aside and grabbing her hand.

"No!" she said, unwilling to budge. "I'll not leave her to the abuse of that madman!"

Alister hesitated, and then nodded. Evelyn knew that they all needed to get away, but she feared that if she left Susan now, Lord Craven would do unspeakable things to her.

"Fine," Alister said as he got to his feet. "Just stay back. Get ready to run."

Evelyn nodded.

Alister wasted no time. He knew he had the element of surprise. He pushed through the crowd and tackled his father, knocking him to the ground and the dagger out of his hand, which slid across the room.

"You insolent brat!" Lord Craven howled as the two struggled. "I should have killed you as I did all my other children!"

The cultists then began to panic, running around in a frenzy. Some tried to continue the ceremony while others fled up the stairs. Some went after Alister, trying to pull him off of Lord Craven. Alister was able to fight some of them off, but there were too many of them.

But none of them seemed to see Evelyn. She slipped through the crowd in the chaos and grabbed the dagger. She then ran to Susan's side.

"M'lady!" Susan gasped. "Help me!"

"Of course," Evelyn said as she started to use the knife to cut the ties. But then she heard Alister grunt. She looked over and saw that several of the cultists were holding Alister's arms. His father was standing before him and punched him in the stomach.

"You will not stop me, child!" Lord Craven roared. He then began to chant something. Alister grunted again, as though fighting an invisible force.

If Evelyn did not see it with her own eyes, she wouldn't have believed it, but she thought that Lord Craven must have been performing the spell to allow him to leap into Alister's body right then! Alister was fighting it, but he was losing. Evelyn could see that his body was starting to go limp.

She couldn't let that happen! She gripped the dagger tightly and ran toward Lord Craven. His back was to her, and he was wearing a thick robe. She knew she had to stab him in the heart to kill him, but she needed to hurt him before he ever saw her or he would overpower her. She raised the dagger high and stabbed him in the back of the neck.

Lord Craven screamed in pain and raised his hands to his wound. Evelyn stepped back, pulling the knife out with her. Blood spurted forth and Lord Craven turned to her with terror in his eyes.

"You..." he rasped. "You were supposed to save me... You...found the words..."

"I'll never be used for evil again!" she screamed as she ran toward him and stabbed him in the neck. "That is for my father!" Lord Craven fell to his knees. She then pulled the dagger out and then stabbed him again. "That is for Hamid!"

As the blood poured out of Lord Craven, the last of his strength seemed to flow out of him as well and he crumbled to the floor.

"I...will...stop...you!" he gurgled as blood began to fill his mouth.

Evelyn pulled his robe open, exposing his chest. "And this is for every person you have ever hurt!" she said as she plunged the dagger into his heart. Then she cited the poetic words from the book.

"*Ida utuk xul lu nakāsu*
Nadānu mâtu u šumul
Rešu ersetu
Birku sinništu sîn kakkabu!"

She didn't know what the words meant, but it didn't seem to matter to the universe, or She of the Moon and Stars, or whatever force was in control. Lord Craven writhed and screamed, and the cultists around them all screamed in pain as well. Then he let out one last guttural moan and went limp, the life completely gone from him. The cultists around them all passed out as well, falling to the floor where they stood.

Alister, freed from the cultists' grips, fell to his knees and gasped for breath. "Evelyn..." he stammered as he tried to breathe.

Evelyn ran to him, falling by his side. "Alister!" she cried. She reached up to touch his face, but realized that her hands were stained with the blood of his father. He recoiled from her touch, falling to his backside.

"What have you done?" he asked.

CHAPTER NINETEEN

*E*velyn and Alister stared at each other, both unable to speak. She had saved their lives, but had killed his father in the process. The cultists around them started to stir. As the rose, they seemed to be in a daze, confused about where they were and what they were doing. One by one they shed their robes and ascended the stairs out of the crypt.

"M...M'lady!" Susan finally stammered, calling Evelyn back to her senses. Evelyn left Alister and ran to Susan's side.

"Are you all right?" Evelyn asked her as she used the cursed dagger that she was still gripping to slash through Susan's bindings.

Susan nodded, but as she tried to stand, she nearly collapsed into Evelyn's arms. "I was so scared!" she cried. "I thought I was going to be raped and dead."

Evelyn held Susan tightly to her chest and shushed her. She didn't have the heart to tell her that she very nearly was the victim of a millennia-old evil spirit.

"You're safe now," Evelyn said. "Let's get out of here."

Evelyn led Susan to the top of the stairs. The morning sun was just starting to shine, reflecting off the crystalline frost on the grass. She picked up her cape by the entrance to the crypt and wrapped it around Susan's shoulders. They could see some of the cultists heading toward the house and many others running through the surrounding fields, undoubtedly returning to their own homes. What would they think? Would they remember anything? Did they see Evelyn kill old Lord Craven?

Evelyn blew out a breath and shook her head. She couldn't think about that right now. She needed to get Susan to safety. Though at the moment, she didn't know where safety was. They certainly wouldn't feel safe in Carnarvon Castle.

"Evelyn!" Alister called out, running up behind them.

"Stay back!" Evelyn said, not slowing her pace as she led Susan forward.

"Just listen to me," he said, running up to her side. She dared not look at him for fear her resolve would waver. At the moment, she didn't know what to think or who to believe. She only knew she needed to get out of this place.

"I can't," Evelyn said. "I need to go. *We* need to go. If you were smart, you'd set explosives to that crypt and then flee this place yourself."

"That's not a terrible idea," he said as they approached the front of the house. "Come inside and warm yourselves by the fire. I'll have Mrs. Paxton bring some tea."

"We are not stepping one foot inside that house," Evelyn said. "There is evil here. We are going home."

"I'll go with you then," Alister said. "Just let me have the coach readied—"

"No," Evelyn said firmly. "I can't see you now. I can't see

this place. I can't ride in your coach. We will walk if we must."

She then turned Susan toward the driveway leading to the main road, but Susan stumbled. Evelyn looked down and saw that Susan wasn't wearing any shoes. Of course she wasn't. She hadn't been wearing anything other than her nightshift when she was tied to the table, but in her haste to escape, Evelyn had forgotten. But Susan had not complained about walking across the freezing yard nearly naked and exhausted. Susan never raised a fuss about anything. Evelyn forced herself to stop and think for a moment. To consider Susan's needs.

"Do you...Are you comfortable going inside?" Evelyn asked her. "Tell me what to do."

"Oh no, m'lady," Susan said. "I just want to go home. To your home. I couldn't face my mother right now."

Evelyn nodded, but still didn't move. She couldn't force Susan to walk in her condition.

"The cat," Susan said. "Can Lord Craven send the cat down to us? She never hurt nobody."

Evelyn nearly winced in pain at the mention of Lord Craven, but then she remembered that Susan was referring to Alister. She was going to have a hard time separating Alister from his father for as long as he had to use the same title.

"Can you bring the cat down?" Evelyn finally asked, chancing a glance at Alister for the first time since the crypt. What she saw on his face nearly broke her heart. He was hurting, both for what he had experienced and for the fact that she was leaving him. But she couldn't take care of everyone right now. Her priority had to be Susan. Then, if she had any energy left, she would care for herself. "Please," she finally added as gently as she could.

Alister nodded as he opened the front door of the house and called for Mrs. Paxton. Mrs. Paxton appeared, looking confused and disheveled.

"Yes, sir?" she asked as she attempted to pat her hair into place.

"Will you please go to Miss Crowley's room and retrieve her cat?" Alister asked her.

"Miss who her what?" Mrs. Paxton asked as though she didn't understand the simple command he had just given.

"Miss Crowley's cat," Alister said, and Mrs. Paxton just shook her head. "The woman right here, Miss Crowley. The woman who has been staying with us for the last several months."

"I swear I never saw that woman in my life before now," Mrs. Paxton said.

Evelyn and Alister glanced at each other. Was it possible that none of the cultists remembered anything from before Lord Craven had taken over their minds? She supposed it was possible. Who knew just how much power the man had. She shrugged.

"Forget it," Alister said. "Just go to the main guest room on the second floor. You'll find a small cat. Bring it."

Mrs. Paxton pressed her lips but then gave a small curtsey as she went back inside.

"And send someone out to prepare the carriage," Alister called after her.

"I'm not getting into your carriage," Evelyn stated again. The thought of being in any enclosed space that was in anyway connected to Lord Craven was too frightening to consider.

"You can't walk back to town," Alister said, growing exasperated. "And you can't stand here in the cold. Susan will freeze to death."

"Sir?" one of the grooms said as came around the side of the house.

"Prepare my—" Alister started to say, but Evelyn cut him off.

"Horse," she said. "Prepare a horse. We will ride home. I'll send it back later."

The groom looked to Alister, who nodded his approval, and the man ran off. Alister then walked close to Evelyn.

"Please," he tried one more time. "I beg of you, come inside. Let's talk. We can't let...whatever just happened go by without remark."

Evelyn shook her head. "I can't. I can't even fathom what just happened, much less remark on it. I need to go home."

Alister frowned and shook his head, but he seemed as at a loss for words as Evelyn. They had both suffered tremendously, but they couldn't lean on each other lest they both fall.

The groom came back around the side of the house leading a horse. Evelyn climbed upon it first, then pulled Susan up behind her. She let Susan keep her cape, even though she was now feeling the biting December chill herself. Her fear and urgency to be away from this place kept her warm. Mrs. Paxton came out of the house holding the cat. Alister took it from her and walked up to the horse and handed it gingerly up to Susan. Susan took the kitten and wrapped it her cloak against her chest. As Alister's hand fell, it brushed Evelyn's foot and she gasped at the spark of electricity she felt course through her. She felt tears well up in her eyes and saw them reflected in Alister's. But she would not give in. She would not stay. She turned the horse out and left Alister—and Carnarvon Castle—behind.

*E*velyn's housekeeper, kitchen maid, cook, and footman were shocked at the sudden return of their mistress and her maid and the state they were in. But Evelyn couldn't tell them what had happened. She only ordered the fires to be lit and for Susan to be placed into a guest room very near her own room so she could keep an eye on her. Susan was given a warm bath, hot soup, and clean clothes, then she was placed in a comfortable bed with her cat to keep her company. Evelyn checked the windows of Susan's room herself three times to make sure they were tightly secured. She thought she would be checking every lock in the house multiple times every night for the foreseeable future.

Only once she was satisfied that Susan was safe and sound did she take a moment for herself. She did not have anyone help her undress; she couldn't stand the feeling of being vulnerable and exposed. As she removed her dress, she was shocked at how much blood had stained the front of it. She tossed the dress to the side to be burned later. She removed the remaining layers and then sank into a hot bath. She vigorously scrubbed the blood from her hands, then from her neck and face that she didn't realize was there. She was lucky her servants hadn't sent for the police. But they were loyal to her.

As the heat seeped into her bones, she tried to reconcile what had happened in her mind. Had they really nearly all been killed by a five-thousand-year-old monster? It seemed at once both preposterous and the only logical explanation. Once she was warm, she forced herself to stand and dress. She had only finished plaiting her hair when there was a knock at the door.

"An Alister Shaw to see you, ma'am," the housekeeper said.

Evelyn couldn't help but smirk to herself at Alister using his given name instead of his title. He must have known how the title unnerved her.

"I'll be right down," Evelyn said, even though she should have had him dismissed without granting him an audience. No, she couldn't do that to him. He was suffering as well, and probably didn't have a close friend to lean on the way she had Susan.

She found him in the parlor, staring into the fire, worrying his thumbnail in his mouth. She had never seen him so anxious.

"Alister," she said, and as he looked at her, his face instantly brightened. He ran to her and she could tell he wanted to embrace her, but her face warned him away. She wasn't ready.

"Forgive me," he said. "I...I just had to see you."

"I know," she said. "That's why I came down. Though I am only here to tell you that we cannot see each other anymore."

His face dropped and his heart was broken. She knew it was a cruel thing to do at this moment when he had already lost so much, but she couldn't give him false hope.

"I can't look at you right now without...remembering..." she said, tears threatening. "I only want to forget."

"I understand," he said. "You cannot comprehend how much I wish I could completely erase my father from my memory."

He then turned away from her and paced the room a few times. He seemed to be searching for the right words to say to her.

"I knew my father was eccentric," he finally said. "And he was always cruel. For the whole of my life, he was a bad father. I know everything with him changed after he came back from Persia with that damn book, but honestly, his demeanor toward me didn't worsen. He was always a cold, hateful person."

Evelyn only nodded and let him unburden himself.

"But I had no idea about the curse or the...the demon. The evil king. Whatever that *thing* inside him was," he said. "I hadn't even seen him for at least five years before he called me home a few months ago, telling me he was dying. He said his last wish was to have the book translated. He had tried to translate it himself all this time, but he had failed. And now he was at death's door. He said he had seen you at the museum, knew of your skills, but he couldn't approach you himself. He said that if you saw his face, if you knew who he was, that you would refuse the job."

Evelyn realized that it must have been Lord Craven who had been watching her at the museum all those months ago. And from the alley across from the Savoy. She knew that whoever it was who had been stalking her had an evil presence.

"He was probably right about that," Evelyn said. "If I had made the connection between the book and my father's death sooner, I never would have accepted the job."

Alister stepped toward her and gripped her hands. "I will never stop asking for your forgiveness in deceiving you about my father being alive. But that was the only lie I knowingly told you. I thought it was just another one of his eccentricities. I never imagined he wished you or Susan or even me any harm. The rest was truth." He reached up and cupped her cheek in his hand. "Especially the part about me loving you."

Evelyn's resolve fractured in that moment and a few

tears slipped down her cheeks. She kissed the palm of his hand. "I believe you," she said.

A small smile of hope crossed his face.

"But," she said before he could think they had any chance of a reconciliation. "But that doesn't mean I can be with you. I am still terrified. Confused. Even a little angry. My mind is running in circles. I don't know who I can trust or what to believe."

"Trust me," Alister said, but Evelyn shook her head.

"Maybe someday," she said. "But not now. I need time. Time to think. Time to heal. I need to take care of Susan. I need...I don't even know what I need other than time to figure things out."

Alister finally nodded. "I understand. I hate it because I love you, but I understand. My family has done you a great harm. As the only living member of my family now, I must be the one to atone for that."

"Please," Evelyn pleaded. "Don't berate yourself unduly. We both played our part in this—wittingly or unwittingly. We both need time to heal—alone."

Alister took her face in his hands and kissed her hard, passionately. With a desperate need. And she met his kiss with equal vigor. There was a low growl in his throat as he forced himself to pull away.

"We will see each other again, Evelyn Crowley," he said. "I promise you."

But before she could respond, he let her go and fled the room. As she heard the front door of the house slam shut, she collapsed on a nearby couch and let herself fall apart, sobbing more freely than she had in years.

CHAPTER TWENTY

Four months later...

"So you see, Evelyn," Henry said as he pulled a new Egyptian artifact out of a box, "the translation of the vase by Davidan is much better than the one by Matthias, which is what I told the board, but they can't tell one from the other."

Evelyn gritted her teeth and nodded as she cataloged the item he handed her. She had found Davidan's translation to be riddled with errors and show a basic lack of understanding, but she knew that if she wanted to continue "volunteering" at the museum, she would have to shut her mouth and agree with anything Henry said.

But Evelyn's placating nature seemed to irritate Henry more than please him.

"Don't you agree, Evelyn?" Henry asked, forcing her to respond.

She paused and gave him a long look. She could see beads of sweat appear on his brow. But finally, she smiled sweetly. "That is why you are head of the department," she said. "To make the hard choices."

Henry sighed, both in annoyance and relief. The tension between them was palatable. It was as though they both knew a confrontation between them was coming, but neither knew when. But while Evelyn seemed content to put the fight off for as long as possible, Henry wanted to get it over with, poking and prodding her at every opportunity.

Evelyn had taken every ounce of pride and self-worth she had and stuffed it into a little corner of her heart, vowing to lock it away in order to return to the museum and ask Henry for the opportunity to volunteer again. She had tried not to. Tried being content at home. But she couldn't. After Susan recovered and life got back to normal, Evelyn was bored. Restless. Her mind needed to be active.

And she needed a distraction to keep from running back to Alister.

She wanted to return to him. To message him. To kiss him. To find comfort in his embrace. But as the weeks turned into months, she feared she had missed her chance. Though, he had made no effort to contact her either. It seemed their love had been passionate in the moment, but was fleeting. A pleasant moment in her life that she would treasure for the rest of her days but was not meant to stand the test of time.

So, she had returned to the museum. Both to occupy her mind and her time. Henry balked at the idea at first, forcing her to apologize and acknowledge his brilliant way of decoding the vase. They never spoke of the fact that his work—which was poorly done—was based on her original discoveries. But Evelyn lorded her superior skills over him in another way—by denying him her translation assistance. She would catalog and research items, but when it came to deciphering any written materials, she deferred to Henry, no matter how wrong he was. And that seemed to be having the desired effect of annoying him to no end.

"Some new Sumerian artifacts arrived yesterday," Henry said, trying a new tack. "I thought you might be interested in cataloging them this afternoon."

"Of course," she said. "As soon as I am done here."

"There is quite a bit of high Sumerian carved into them," he went on. "If you could include the translations with your catalog notes it would be appreciated."

"I think you mean *transcribe*," Evelyn said coolly as she kept working, not looking at him. "So that we can send them to a real, college-educated translator to work on deciphering them. I can do that, of course."

Out of the corner of her eye, she could see Henry staring at her, the vein in his forehead pulsing. But Evelyn would not give him the satisfaction of looking at him. Of giving his displeasure an audience. If he had thought that by taking her back he could once again use her language abilities to elevate his own position, he was surely mistaken. She might have had to humble herself in order to return to the museum, but never again would she allow him—or any man—to use her so shamelessly.

"Of course, that is what I meant," Henry finally said, returning to unpacking a box. The storm, once again, abated—for now.

"Ah! Henry!" a jovial voice said. "And Lady Sommers." It was Lord Clifford, one of the top members of the museum's board of directors.

"My lord," Henry said, approaching the elderly man and shaking his hand. Evelyn then gave the man a curtsey, which he repaid with a small bow.

"Just the two people I wanted to see," Lord Clifford said.

He was smiling, but Evelyn noticed his hand was shaking a bit as though he had a touch of nerves. "I have some rather exciting news."

"Oh?" Henry asked. "Do tell."

"The museum has acquired a new very—and I mean *very*—generous patron," Lord Clifford said. "Thanks to him, we won't need to do any fundraising for years to come. Of course, we will continue to do so, but that is just to give you an idea of how important this new patron is."

"That's wonderful news!" Henry said. "There is so much we could do with funds like that."

"Yes, yes," Lord Clifford said, his eyes shifting away from Henry. "But...I'm afraid it does come with a bit of a catch." He looked at Evelyn.

Henry's gaze followed Lord Clifford's and the smile ran from his face. "What...what does Evelyn have to do with anything?"

Evelyn's nostrils flared at his use of her given name in front of the lord. Lord Clifford seemed to take offense at Henry's lack of respect toward her as well, which bolstered him to continue.

"The new patron's donation comes with a stipulation," Lord Clifford explained. "He will only release the funds when *Lady Sommers* is made the curator of the Near East and North African departments."

"What?" Henry and Evelyn said at the same time, but their tones could not have been more different. Henry's voice was laced with anger while Evelyn's was shocked.

"It did seem an odd request," Lord Clifford said, "but we all know that Lady Sommers is qualified, by virtue of her experience if not credentials."

"That's ridiculous," Henry said. "She can't even *work*

here, but you are just going to give her the entire department?"

"I will remind you, Mr. Wilkes," Lord Clifford said, "that the board has always been open to giving Lady Sommers a proper position. It has been you who has insisted that she remain as merely a volunteer."

"Henry!" Evelyn gasped. "Is this true?"

"I...That's...My lord—" Henry stammered, but Lord Clifford cut him off.

"We all appreciate the work you have done here, Henry," Lord Clifford said. "But we all know that the quality of your translations—the initial discovery of the vase notwithstanding—have diminished significantly over the last year or so. Nearly any person—man or woman—who has spent time overseas can find errors in your translations."

Evelyn did her best not to smile at that.

"Of course," Lord Clifford went on, "we would prefer a man with both a university education and Miss Crowley's experience and practical skills, but we can't have everything."

"Are you firing me?" Henry finally asked.

"Well, I suppose that will be up to the new department curator," Lord Clifford said, looking at Evelyn with a gleam in his eye.

"I...I hardly know what to say." Evelyn was ecstatic really. It was like a dream. But she knew she needed to get more information before she could accept. "Who is this new patron? Who could possibly have that much faith in me?"

"That would be me." Alister walked into the room as though waiting for his cue. Well, *swaggered* into the room would be more accurate, swinging his walking stick, his topper at a jaunty angle.

Evelyn's heart leaped at seeing him. She had wondered what she would do, think, and feel when she saw him again. They left on the most disappointing of terms. But now that the moment had come, she only wanted to run into his arms. She resisted the urge, of course, but she could not hide the smile that infected her lips.

"I should have known!" Henry exclaimed. "Lord Clifford, you cannot allow them to conspire against me! They are lovers!"

"How dare you!" Lord Clifford said. "You should think twice before you slander your betters. This is the second time you have tried to publicly defame Lady Sommers. For that alone I should toss you out on your ear."

"Please," Evelyn said. "Let us all calm down. This is shocking news. I think we should all take a moment to breathe before speaking further. And I would wish for a chance to learn all the details about the position before making a decision."

"So my entire life is now in her hands?" Henry asked Lord Clifford.

"It seems only fair," Evelyn answered. "Apparently you have been holding my life in yours for quite some time."

"This is an outrage!" Henry said as he pushed past Alister and left the room. They all watched him leave, not sorry to see the back of him.

"I do hope your first act as head of the department is to give that boy his dismissal notice," Lord Clifford said to Evelyn.

"I don't want to do anything rash," she said, and she meant it. She was serious about talking to Alister about the details of the arrangement before agreeing to anything.

"Of course, my dear," Lord Clifford said. "It is a big decision, a large responsibility. Take all the time you need.

Come see me at my home when you have an answer for me." With that, he doffed his hat to Evelyn and Alister and then left.

Evelyn and Alister looked at each other with large smiles on their faces, but they didn't speak. It was as though they had not almost been killed by a five-thousand-year-old demon and were just two people in love who had been missing each other immensely. Speaking would shatter that façade.

"I do hope that saying you needed time to think about the offer was only for Henry's benefit," Alister finally said. "Surely you plan to accept."

"I did enjoy seeing his face turn red," Evelyn admitted. "But given our...history, I do think we need to be very specific about the terms of my employment should I accept."

"Perhaps we can discuss it over dinner," Alister said.

Evelyn shook her head. "That would be...a bit too intimate," she said. "But, the weather outside is beautiful. Perhaps we could walk through the park?"

Alister could not hide that he was disappointed she had declined his offer for dinner, but he happily and graciously offered her his arm.

"I would be delighted," he said.

It was mid-morning and early spring. There was a slight chill in the air, but Evelyn was warmed by Alister's mere presence as they strolled arm-in-arm through a park nearby. Evelyn bought a small bag of seeds to feed to the ducks and other birds who were already returning from their sojourn south.

"You seem rather subdued," Alister said. "I thought you would be more excited to finally be working at the museum properly."

"It's all just a bit overwhelming, I suppose," she said as they stopped by the edge of the pond and she threw some seeds in the water. "Did you know I had returned to the museum before you became a patron."

"We haven't spoken since that day at your house," Alister said. "But I have kept an eye on you. I was surprised when you went back, but I thought it was a good sign you were moving on."

"I don't have much choice," she said. "Susan is getting married soon. If her new husband doesn't find a placement in London, she will leave me. The world keeps spinning and I must find my place on it or risk being cast adrift."

"And is your place at the museum, Madam Curator?" Alister asked with a chuckle.

Evelyn let out a small laugh as well. "That does have a nice ring to it. But I'm not sure. I never imagined such a thing would be possible."

"Evelyn," Alister said, taking her hand. "Anything is possible. You are young, smart, beautiful, wealthy. You need to stop thinking in terms of what you can't do and imagine what you can. If you could do anything in this world, what would you do right now?"

Evelyn knew the answer to that question the moment he asked, but she hesitated because she knew it was not the answer he would want to hear and she didn't want to hurt him. She remembered her resolve to always be honest with him, though, and spoke.

"I would leave England," she said, and his face fell. She forced herself to continue. "I want to return to Persia. That is where my heart and I believe my home is. At least for a while. I was forced to leave before I was ready. And I would give anything to go back."

"Then you should go," Alister said, even though it hurt

him to do so, she could see in his eyes. "You could go on the museum's behalf. Collect items and improve your translation skills. Then you can come back and serve as curator when you are ready."

That was certainly appealing to her. Not just traveling as a tourist—or hobbyist—but as a researcher, a museum curator. It would give her so much more authority when dealing with other people.

"I can't go alone, though," she said. "It's far too dangerous for a woman. Not to mention lonely."

"You wouldn't have to travel alone," Alister said, squeezing her hand, "if you married me."

Her heart nearly exploded in her chest at his words. It was all she ever wanted. The man she loved and living in the country she loved. It was a dream. She bit the inside of her cheek to make sure she wasn't asleep.

"Are you sure?" she asked slowly. "Even after...everything?" She didn't want to remind him that it was she who stabbed his father in the chest, but it was a fact that couldn't —and shouldn't—be ignored. If they didn't speak plainly about it now, any resentment he might feel for her, no matter how small, could fester and grow only to explode later.

"That man," Alister said, "was not my father. My father died the day he found that book. You saved my life, Evelyn. For that, and for a hundred other reasons, I love you and want to make you my wife."

Evelyn laughed and happy tears pooled in her eyes. "It will be a very unusual life. A wife traveling for work and a husband following behind. Are you sure you would be able to stand it?"

"What aspect of our lives has ever been normal?" Alister

asked. "I wouldn't want an ordinary life with you. How boring!"

"I do have one condition," she said.

"Only one?" he asked.

"Well, one to start," she said. "You will hire Susan's betrothed as your valet."

"Consider it done," he said without hesitation.

"Then...I accept!" she said.

"The job or the marriage proposal?" Alister asked.

"Both!" she said.

They embraced and kissed, in full view of anyone who could see them.

The End

I hope you enjoyed *The Sumerian Curse*. Never miss a new release by subscribing to my newsletter.
http://leighandersonromance.com/subscribe/

ABOUT THE AUTHOR

 Leigh Anderson loves all things Gothic and paranormal. She did her master's thesis on vampire imagery in Gothic novels and met her husband while assuming the role of a vampire online. She currently teaches writing at several universities and has a rather impressive collection of tiny hats. She lives in a small town in the mountains where she raises bearded dragons and gives them wings for Halloween. She is currently working on too many writing projects, and yet not enough.

Sign up for her mailing list and stalk her around the web to keep in touch and be the first to learn about new releases.

Newsletter: http://leighandersonromance.com/subscribe/
Facebook: https://www.facebook.com/LeighAndersonRomance/
Twitter: https://twitter.com/LeighA_Romance/
Goodreads: https://www.goodreads.com/leighanderson
Bookbub: https://www.bookbub.com/authors/leigh-anderson-755d218b-1d7b-4aa2-97f9-427cb3c12f98
Instagram: https://www.instagram.com/leigh_anderson_romance/

ABOUT THE PUBLISHER

VISIT OUR WEBSITE
TO SEE ALL OF OUR HIGH QUALITY BOOKS:

http://www.redempresspublishing.com

Quality trade paperbacks, downloads, audio books, and books in foreign languages in genres such as historical, romance, mystery, and fantasy.